Temper

PHOEBE WALKER

Fairlight Books

First published by Fairlight Books 2023

Fairlight Books
Summertown Pavilion, 18–24 Middle Way, Oxford, OX2 7LG

Copyright © Phoebe Walker 2023

The moral right of Phoebe Walker to be identified as the author of this work has been asserted by Phoebe Walker in accordance with the Copyright, Designs and Patents Act 1988.

All rights reserved. This book is copyright material and must not be copied, stored, distributed, transmitted, reproduced or otherwise made available in any form, or by any means (electronic, digital, optical, mechanical, photocopying, recording or otherwise) without the prior written permission of the publisher.

A CIP catalogue record for this book is available from the British Library

1 2 3 4 5 6 7 8 9 10

ISBN 978-1-914148-28-6

www.fairlightbooks.com

Printed and bound in Great Britain

Designed by Anna Morrison

This is a work of fiction. Names, characters, businesses, events and incidents are the products of the author's imagination. Any resemblance to actual persons, living or dead, or actual events is purely coincidental.

For Sam

Autumn

Life in slow motion, I think. Then I think severely, that is pedestrian, and beneath you. Every morning he kisses me, the knot of his tie on my forehead, and I say,

Have fun and be yourself.

And he leaves. Much later, hours and hours sometimes, I get up and wash at the basin, under a small window open to the cooling air, then go downstairs to make coffee. I peel an orange and stare at my screen. Sometimes I am full of purpose, answering emails and arranging calls, tap tap. I look up dance classes and swimming timetables, day trips, festivals, restaurants. I've never tried Nepalese cuisine, never visited the Christmas markets at Cologne, now only four hours away by train.

I search for recipes by a single ingredient: glass noodles, pinto beans, courgette, honey, cashews. At 3pm, I eat mounded handfuls of speculoos biscuits, which here come shaped like macarons and are covered in milk chocolate. I marvel at myself.

It's the smoking that gets me out of the house.

*

Today we had a thunderstorm. I've rarely experienced a storm in the morning, before the bins have even been taken, and I enjoy it, the early havoc of light and coarse rain.

I am so stupid here. I go into a shop and pick up the sort of things a woman like me picks up: hair mousse, satsumas, hand cream, linseed crackers, carnations. At the till the (invariable) woman smiles and says—

And I stare and say, Sorry? I even put a craven inflection on it, Zhorry, to make it sound as if I am possibly not English, and so worthy of a little more patience. And then she repeats what she has said in immaculate English, and I say Aha, and pay. Usually, she is just asking about coupons, or plastic bags. Zhorry.

*

I can't get away from this internal posturing, desperate, like someone turning endlessly in front of a department store mirror, piping, and from this side? and this side? with terrified eyes.

There's a gap where my sense of place should be. It's quite a useful one sometimes. It allows me to sit on the cusp of an opinion. I can nod along when people around me say: Of course, here they have a different way of doing things, and not all of it is done well; their record on the things they're fêted for actually lags way behind – *way* behind – their European counterparts; it's not all tolerance and equality, it's not all plain speaking. And environmentally? Well, count all the bikes you like, they're not doing half of what Sweden, Norway, Germany are doing; they're actually a big polluter, relatively speaking. But you won't get anywhere talking to any of them about that.

And then, when others say to me: You must be so happy not to be in the UK any more. I mean, everyone I know wants to get out. It's all austerity, splendid isolation, permanent crisis. It gets worse, every week it gets worse. Whereas, here – well, you've just got to look around you: the libraries, the parks, the public transport, the schools, the recycling, the municipal flower displays! Everything just works. They really have nailed, *nailed*, their civic infrastructure. You won't want to go back, after a year or two here. I mean, you're not planning on it, are you?

I agree to all of this, at different times. Sometimes I'm the one saying this – or at least, saying certain phrases – the way when I lived in London I agreed that it was a relief to live among so much culture, energy, the buzz of the city; and when I returned north, to the half-abandoned fringe of coast on which I'd grown up, to the friends who hadn't left, I said how wonderful it was to have space, to have quiet, to pay a sensible price for a pint.

Here, this is less tact than diffidence, but it leaves me feeling unaffiliated, drifting aimlessly in the void between two countries, with no predilection, no plan for movement towards one or the other. And you can choose, I tell myself sourly, to go either way. What fortune, to be able to base a choice on liking, to be worried only about the lack of it. Here, the Netherlands, with its seeming ease and order, is the least complicated place we could have come to. I am well aware of this: that this is the tamest and most tepid flight we could have made.

*

It was hot today, the last gasp before the cooler weather sets in. I felt at a loss. I'd know how to feel in this weather at home, I think – what my plans would be, who they'd be with. Heat and light bring to mind yellow grass, hasty plans, swoops onto the chiller cabinets of express supermarkets, emerging from damp train carriages, spilling like blood through the sutures of the bus, knowing there are glowing hours ahead. The heat would be in me, and around me, unaccustomed warmth in my mind, beneath my skin. Here, I experienced the heat only as something physical, something practical. I changed my outfit, stuck my bare foot into a patch of sunlight on the sofa. There was nobody to call.

*

How's it going? Where's it going? I know Robin gets asked things like this by his colleagues, whose minds run in these nevertheless life-affirming channels. He works for a company that manufactures all kinds of foodstuffs, its logo found everywhere from baby food to biscuits. His career was the engine of our move here. The granular nature of work in this kind of megacorp is incredible: his job involves keeping a close eye on the global supply of seeds and legumes. I went to a drinks reception at his offices this week, to welcome newcomers, and was greeted immediately by a woman, a stranger, who said to me: We have heard so much! And we will get him to marry you! She heaped my plate with four skewers of chicken, dunked in satay sauce. After I had eaten one, the same woman leant over my shoulder and said blandly: No one should eat so much meat in one day.

I'm forgetting what it's like to have colleagues. It's such a con, I tell people bravely, the nine-to-five, the forty-hour week. Since I've started freelancing, since I've been working for myself, by myself, I get a day's work done in four hours – less! Nobody is interested in hearing this, they smile and mime envy, but it invites no interest, no genuine sense that this is something to be desired. And maybe they're right. My spare hours do stack up aimlessly, slabs of white-walled afternoon spent topping up my water glass. Footsteps in the street bring me soundlessly to the window, like a cat, to watch others, busier than myself, recede purposefully in the direction of the city.

A woman, one of our neighbours, came to collect a parcel that had been left at our house. She introduced herself as Suzanne and, looking at me closely, invited me to join her at her house – 7b, just a few doors down – for a cup of tea or a glass of wine sometime. It's good to know your neighbours, she added. We both know the chances of this invitation ever being taken up are close to zero. I imagined knocking on her door one Monday evening, slyly brandishing a bottle of red. I imagined what we'd talk about: her family, her work, my infinitely more slender grasp on both, both of us silently wondering what the other is doing here: Suzanne, in my company, and me, in her country, doing very little for one another.

*

Our landlady came today to check the fire alarms. She insisted on explaining to me the history of the house and of its street, the point of which seemed to be that we are fortunate enough to find ourselves living in a real-life *Upstairs Downstairs*, occupying the space that once would have held servants' quarters. *Downton Abbey*! she said, and moved as if to nudge me. I went to tuck a lamp's trailing cable behind a drawer, and she immediately made some minute adjustment to it, then said, It's as you prefer, of course.

*

I scalded my soup today, again, and spent ten minutes scraping potato sludge from the pan. Food is on my mind, of course. The past afternoon I spent with other women, colleagues of Robin's, or partners of his colleagues. After half an hour the sticky ball of conversation rolled, predictably, around to food. It started as a veiled interest in other people's health. What gym do people go to? one person asked. What classes are others signed up for? Someone said they did spin, because it gave them a higher resting metabolism. Means I can do this more, she said, picking out a doughnut from an untouched box that lay on the table, taking a ceremonious bite.

One woman asked if that really worked. Someone else said it didn't for them. They had to watch what they ate like a hawk. And it hadn't always been like that. Up till about my mid-twenties, she told us, I could eat what I liked. And drink whatever, I was out every night. Almost.

There was a collective sigh of nostalgia, then it was on to personal strategies, laid out and coyly compared, larded with cries of, Oh you are *good*; Oh, I'd never have that much self-control! Dinners replaced by palmfuls of fish fingers, baked dark brown to leach out the excess oil. The cloudy procession of Tupperware, the plastic shrunk to almost purposeless dimensions, but in fact fit for holding one slender branch of grapes, or six almonds, or a tablespoon of quark, to be enjoyed mid-morning. I mustered my own contributions, half-heartedly: the years of sugarless jellies, the carob-coated raisins, and received a series of knowing nods from the others.

I said all this, despite knowing full well that with friends, with family, I happily play the glutton. I demand a third portion, a fourth. I dip my spoon, with apologies, into the central pot; I fish out nuggets of meat and swallow them with audible relish. I hover beside the dishwasher, spooning alternate helpings of dry rice and stock juices into my mouth. I abhor waste, I say loudly, food waste is a sin. Any left? Pass it down! is a common cry at communal dinners, and I grin and beckon it on, and I load my plate, and I fill my mouth.

And despite the glee of our selective sharing, the communal release of breath, I knew that the personal and collective fictions would remain upheld: there would be no deeper probing, no unearthing of our genuine unease. We'd continue visiting each other's houses, sitting down on imitation-leather sofas in front of a painstakingly chosen spread: four-cheese pizzas, crispbreads and two types of hummus, olives. At intervals a timer would go, and our hostess would run to unearth another garlic bread, a tray of quick-bake spring rolls, and dump them on the heap. Our fingers would fidget in the packets, among the olives. God, I can't stop, we'd say. Someone take it away from me.

*

I have a new haircut and it gives me an austere aspect. There's something curt and efficient about it that suggests a character at odds with my present indolence. I am dressed mostly in black today, with severe geometric earrings, and I think this completes the look. I have the appearance of an early-career architect – when I wore this same outfit to my Dutch language class, weeks ago, the teacher in fact asked if I was a graphic designer. I felt a moment's pride, at becoming such a consummate blank slate for someone else's projections, which are as good as, in fact better than, my own.

To go with the haircut, I've been buying clothes this week, feeling only partially guilt-ridden at the money I've spent on myself. I tried everything on upstairs in the bedroom (first drawing the blind against the painters propped up on scaffolding at the neighbouring house), and had twenty minutes silent gloating over my fragile-seeming collarbone. I have moments like this every few months or so, or after new purchases, and it sends me conjuring up impressive entrances at parties, which so rarely explode from fantasy into reality. On any such occasion, overdressed or underdressed – or just plainly dressed – is my usual feeling. Even my hair (which I can imagine to be falling in just the right way across my temples) proves, on closer inspection in the toilets, to be traitorously slanting at random, stray hairs streaked over my ears.

I have to be careful, though, not to let things slip, let things slide. On weekdays, I keep leaving the house without brushing my teeth, feeling the grimy fuzz against my tongue. Wearing the same clothes a few days running, not bothering to wipe down my keyboard. These are all signals of— what? Some decline, some settling of all the aimless particles of my life? Not yet. Something else – a little malaise, a little busy, petted anxiety? The words have an adult glitter.

The work stays real enough, even when I feel there's not much of it. I write copy, proofread, help people with their marketing strategies. My clients are all in the UK, mostly small and earnest: tiny tech start-ups, restaurants, online boutiques. This is an extension, more or less, of what I used to do in an office, only the clients were larger, the self-importance in direct proportion. I decided to carry it on out of necessity, originally, doubting I'd be able to find a job in a new country straight away, with my lack of language skills and connections. So far, it's worked well enough, as well as I need it to. My clients are tickled to think of me being in a different country; they like the cosmopolitan gleam that 'our colleague in the Netherlands' conjures up, while I draft website banners and piece together newsletters and line up cheery boasts on their social media accounts. Mostly, I don't miss the office. There are some days here when, white-minded with insomnia, it's a relief to just curl myself into a corner of the sofa, typing with one eye open, not having to make conversation.

I find it difficult to explain to others here, to Robin's colleagues, what I do. I say that I work for myself, and they look politely puzzled, cocking their heads slightly to one side, as though their hearing is clouded. 'Business' has a very particular definition here, and it's consequently not a word I use. But, I think crossly, I have done something, am doing something, by myself; steeled for the bureaucracy of another country, another language. Childishly, I want his colleagues to be more impressed with me than they are: I'm doing what none of you are doing, I think sourly, I'm running my own show. And then the thought dissolves: all of it is incidental, we are not here because of me.

Last night I had a message from an old colleague, half-cut at an awards party with no one to talk to – no one to bitch with, she put it. We sparred a little; I was very aware that any time she sent me a longer message it probably meant she was sitting on the toilet, grinning, and I remembered those flushed evenings of my early career, lit by a glamour that was not at all adult, completely unsophisticated. It being a small world and a small industry, the chat and the atmosphere was always spiteful; you had to be aware of the dislikes and enmities and the legendary differences of opinion. You also had to be aware of the wandering hands, the complicit clots of people in which ubiquitous creeps lurked and chattered. At least it made things relevant, I thought then, at least it made me feel worldly, part of something.

*

I'm trying to read some history of this place, but the best and most detailed books in the library are not available in English and I'm unwilling to spend money on the translations. I keep a running accounts book in my head and am, I know, more careful than I need to be (lucky me), but this carefulness has curdled into habit now, so I get as much pleasure from, say, abstaining from the purchase of some lurid new earrings (tortoiseshell! Tasselled! Three euros ninety-nine!) as I would from actually wearing them. I think about money all the time, when I am dragging the towels from the washing machine, or stretching to turn off my alarm in the morning, or walking aimlessly to relentlessly upbeat playlists. It's not charming, this obsession, and not one I turn to with pleasure – nor yet from any real anxiety. It's another of those things that my mind, hanging in the untasted formaldehyde of this new place, finds to prey on, pointlessly. That solution, in which I'm now suspended, should be harmless salt. But I find as time goes on it is more corrosive, and the mind frays and clouds accordingly, refusing to gather. I don't want to imagine where I'll be a year from now.

*

Today I went to a networking event aimed at the city's non-profit organisations. I had a sense of wanting to do something useful with all this new time; and of getting to know the city better through some of its services. The entire building, the conference centre where it was held, reeked of long-baked-in body odour, fusty and brown, a match for the carpets. The presentation room was overcrowded, and harassed-looking centre staff were carrying in armfuls of extra chairs, glaring at those already seated and thrusting them against impractical edges of the room. I sat next to a woman who kept glancing at my programme and letting her eyes linger on me in a way that suggested she would launch into conversation, given encouragement. I kept my eyes averted. The first presentation was overdue, and the causes of this were being narrated by a young woman through a cordless mic. She kept calling people, seemingly at random, up to the front, frequently interrupting her own administrative monologue. The first speech was a lecture on how to be more self-assertive, accompanied by graphs. We were exhorted to consider signing up for one of the speakers' courses afterwards; the woman next to me shouted no, and shifted assertively in her chair; the woman in front turned around and grinned nervously at both of us. I checked my phone.

This was followed by presentations from the charities present, a blur of animal shelters, children's activity centres and refugee resettlement organisations. Several forgot to mention what their charity did at all, or added this as an afterthought before they gratefully handed the microphone back. The compère introduced each new speaker by clapping loudly above her head, a sound which echoed reluctantly around the room. When it was finally over, my neighbour turned to me and asked aggressively which organisation I would be volunteering with. I replied that I hadn't liked the sound of any of them and escaped, collected my coat and wrote some brief and vitriolic feedback on the back of the programme, which I dropped into a glass vase on the front desk.

No good? asked Robin, later, when I told him what the event had been like. I exaggerated the awfulness of it: the diffidence of the speakers, the smell of the room. No good, I said.

*

I had a vague notion of walking out to the coast – an hour on foot both ways. I wanted to feel the pressure of the white sky above me, and watch the sea, its thin tongue of steel. I wanted to be able to tell people back in England what the shoreline here is like, compare it to Brighton, or to Saint Bees; a grain of homing mixed up in my explanation. I wanted to pad along the sand and listen to the saline roar. But no, I didn't go. I sat in our living room, with its very upright chairs, and swathed myself in Robin's dressing gown, not bothering to turn the heating on.

I've discovered that the rooms in this apartment mysteriously change odours, so that sometimes the bathroom smells of stewed garlic, and the living room of sweet, stale blood. When I run my hand along the wall in the kitchen, in the gap between the fridge and the door, my palm comes back shimmering with damp. There's no heat in this room at all, and the floor is thin linoleum, so when I'm cooking I wear thick socks and one of Robin's hoodies, kept permanently on a listing hook on the back of the door. He complained to me last week that it was unwearable now, its fibres permanently ingrained with the smell of onions. I told him that, to me, nothing could smell more alluring.

*

Work, the nature of it, the point of it, the way that it insists on applying structure, dictating meaning. You find your moral purpose in work; some people go on about that, the backwash of old religion. The stigma, the tedium of worklessness. I'm not workless, but my working pace has slowed, here, to a level where I feel itchy. To my surprise, it's been borne out of what I'd chattered about brightly, defensively, to Robin's colleagues: I am putting in fewer hours, seeing more or less the same results. I'm efficient when I have to be; I dispatch the jobs quickly, and then the days hang heavy. I'm being lazy about things, walking the same old routes to the supermarket and the library, neglecting my bike. I could zip around the countryside on the efficient public transport network, I could pummel flat the stodge of my mind. I could meet new people.

Often, I stand staring at the flat opposite, where no one ever appears in the window, and the lights are never on. There has been a dead wasp trapped between the slats of the window blinds for over a fortnight, by my reckoning. If I squint, I can make out the fuzzy texture of its body; I imagine that fuzz being augmented, day by day, by quiet layers of dust.

I mooned today over local volunteering pages, mutual aid associations, community groups. The English translation my browser automatically applies warps the phrasing 'assist us in the spread of courteous notions with our community'. It makes affable notions sound like diseases, cloudy droplets thickening the air. 'Community': always so synonymous with good things; neighbourliness, solidarity, identity, stability. But communities can be malign and exclusive, can be networks of terror, or unchallenged prejudice, or inertia. It makes me wary, my half-hearted attempts to catch on to those threads. Although maybe here, where the whole city is characterised by transience, it has a sort of glossy, frictionless patina. It is as good a place as any to experiment.

*

Already, I'm thinking of winter. Smoke in the air makes me feel things more keenly, as the year turns like a small beast, exposing a shabbier, slept-on hide. I'll miss not having a bonfire here. I feel the lack of flame and fat, the regimented whiff of danger that used to hang about the displays at home. Fireworks are licensed here only on New Year's Eve, I'm warned, although already on some evenings I've heard the pop and bang of illicit firecrackers, familiar to any suburban cul-de-sac.

Punch-drunk, I have to shake my mind to get rid of all that. Or no, that's not quite the right image – rather, I have to let it settle, a fine layer of silt, so fine it is almost greasy, and then be cautious about disturbing it – the odd cheap plink of a thought, the odd cloud of grit – OK. But not the whirlpool, not the filthy, rising tide. I'm sleeping too late, at the moment, feeling so tired, without rationale. It's colder now, the sky always grey and lowering, and we've had bouts of hail already which have sent me hunting for my hat and gloves. On the whole I prefer this; the weather seems to flatter a natural tendency to indolence. It's a relief to draw the curtains at six and shun the possibility of going out. It's a relief to mooch by the radiator and stare at the cat in the window opposite, in turn staring at the oversized pigeons on the balcony. Guests are imminent, and I have lists that instruct me to buy wine, stewing beef, plums, tonic water, lime pickle. I have library books to return and work – real work – to do. I feel curiously like an invalid, cheated of my illness. This feels like a waiting time, which, when I analyse it, is often my experience of these late autumn, early winter days. This is my keenest time of year, growing (I think) from some vague affinity with its malignant undertow, a sense that somehow the membranes of different realities are stretched thinner now, to the point of bloodless breaking.

*

When I said I was moving here, the people in my office said, how exciting, as did my friends, as did my family. Lots of jokes about weed, one or two about the red-light district. Lots of nudges for Robin.

My sister said, I thought you wanted to move really far away, like, really far. It's what's come up, I told her, it's what's available, and we're going to take the chance now. Robin and I had dinner with Shauna and her boyfriend, a few nights before we left, at her flat in Camberwell. She made it obvious that our conversation was boring her, and in fairness it was dull: freight companies and flight arrangements; how we'd left things with our landlord; how we hoped the broken toilet seat wouldn't stop us getting our deposit back. I didn't know how to communicate to her my pure relief at leaving London, a city she loved and had told me, over and over again, that she could never dream of leaving, not permanently. Not for anything. Unasked, Shauna had told us abruptly, in the middle of a conversation about the Eurostar, that her career was here, and she would never get a job as good anywhere else. Never. She was an account manager for a cosmetics company, working long hours, she asserted, with company socials most weeks, and client hospitality at the weekends. I tried telling her that it sounded brilliant, and then teased her that she was going to be the next Kendall Jenner. Don't patronise me, she said, repeatedly, don't patronise.

Her boyfriend talked to Robin doggedly about cricket, then about football, then about boxing; he could never remember that Robin didn't care about sport.

Before I met Robin, I remember the dread of introducing my sister to the people I was dating, which she had always demanded. I can't think, now, why I didn't say no to this. It only happened two or three times, only with people I had been seeing for four months or more. Shauna would always take great care over her outfit, no matter how casual the pub, how brief the meeting. I knew she didn't have a work laptop, but at these occasions she would always be carrying one, in a smart navy case. I caught her once, hovering by the riverside before we were due to meet, pressing a powder pad fiercely against her face. An oily complexion is one thing, at least, that we have in common.

Afterwards – after the drinks and trading of mild opinions, the rolling chat about colleagues and commutes – I'd get a message from Shauna, summarising every perceived slight my date had made, to me or to her, every potential red flag. The people I introduced her to, when I asked how they found her, would just mutter things like, She's formidable. My sister had nicked their consciousness like a coarse needle, leaving them wincing and rubbing the point of impact, eager to forget it.

Since I've moved, we don't speak much. We don't continue any conversations; we don't share any jokes. When we message, we keep to the same rote questions: How is work? How is her boyfriend? Will I see her at Christmas? Would she like to visit, perhaps on the next Bank Holiday weekend? We sometimes talk, in a desultory way, about where we grew up: the north-west coast, in a town whose decay seemed hastened somehow by decades of salt spray, the corrosive screaming of gulls. Shauna had told me once, that when she was older, she wanted to buy a flat there and rent it out. That way, she would have somewhere close to our parents to stay, when it was needed. When I replied that I didn't think buying to let was a particularly moral thing to do, she sent me a string of eye-rolling emojis, then a link to an article about ethical landlords. She'd said to me, not long before we left, We can't all live the corporate wife life, which was as close to any kind of truly energetic argument as we ever got. I don't think you know what you're saying, I'd said to her stiffly, I'm not a wife. Don't patronise, she said.

She hadn't been at home the last few times I visited. My parents knew nothing about her plans to buy a flat there. She doesn't even like it here, my mother said, and why should she? There's nothing here for the young.

*

One of Robin's colleagues asked me if I wanted to join the book group she'd founded, which I duly went to, although the first meeting wasn't that promising. Most of the people there worked at one of the English-language international schools, and the conversation, when it wasn't angled awkwardly towards the book, cantered along on the topic of this school, its executive leadership, the children that attended it. It was forty minutes before we even started to discuss the book, following a prolonged communal gripe about an email sent by the headteacher, which had caused affront. I'm not saying it just because it's her, necessarily, several people repeated, it's what it implies.

The Color Purple, finally. They had all loved it, loved it, brilliant, brilliant. Some of the secondary school teachers went into a huddle: What might Year Ten make of it, did people think? Would some sections be helpful with this part of the curriculum? And then they were off again, into specifications and modelling and phonics, and which staff would be coming on the annual camping trip, and why Delphine had been forced again to buy paper for the staff toilets at lunchtime, when the head had tulips replenished weekly on her desk for everybody to see.

I did go to a serious book group when I lived in London, where we huddled in one another's dampish living rooms, drinking wine and practising quiet conversational one-upmanship about our careers, our relationships, our friends. We met regularly, all through the first autumn and winter that I lived there. One of the women worked for a big confectionery company, and on occasion would come lugging white cardboard boxes filled with the new products that had just finished the development phase, and weren't yet on general release. We all brightened at those colourful packets, the slight unfamiliarity of their contents, endless riffs on the same winningly cheap and chocolatey theme. I often felt pained that my own job had so few perks – even Megan, who worked reluctantly as a receptionist for an obscure art gallery in the suburbs, had occasionally been able to offer us a spare ticket to an undersold show or exhibition that we were too naive to turn down. I had nothing to offer, beyond a little sensationalist gossip about my managers; no expert insight to pass down, no advice to administer; certainly no free seats in corporate boxes, or five-course meals on an expense account.

Once, in my last job before we moved to the Netherlands, I had gone to address a team of PR specialists. It was supposed to be some kind of reverse mentoring thing: small start-ups talking to established companies about what they could learn from those at the bottom of the pile (mostly, that they were glad to be where they were). I was surprised to find that for my twenty-minute, half-hearted presentation, they had ordered a side table of assorted sandwiches, crisps and fruit. They had sparkling water and Coke in slim glass bottles, in an actual ice bucket, and the sandwich fillings included one with crayfish, another with prosciutto.

At the end of my talk, attended by about eight people from their hundred-strong department, the organiser insisted I take the food back with me. We would have nothing like this at our offices (actually, just the one, I corrected him in my head), he was quite sure. He was quite correct. I was embarrassed and exaggeratedly grateful, packing the uneaten sandwiches enthusiastically into brown boxes, and only just drawing the line when he suggested emptying the crisp bowl into a carrier bag. I sent a dreary email round to my colleagues, afterwards, explaining that there were now up to sixty fancy sandwiches in our shared fridge, if anyone cared for them. Later that week I found the same boxes untouched, the crayfish tails slimy and greying, the prosciutto in desiccated shreds.

*

I was sometimes quietly surprised to have ended up, like everyone else, in London. I'd hated even the idea of the city as a child, without being able to trace the reason. On brief visits there, I tensed with angry horror at the crowds and the busyness, feeling each shoulder brush and impatient tut as a personal affront. Standing under the glare of Tube lights as we swayed from Oxford Circus to Notting Hill Gate, I almost wept with a rage for which I could find no rationale. I still can't explain what exactly I found to hate so much, except perhaps to say that some helpless loyalty to home – something I was equally unable to articulate, beyond knowing that home had me in her fierce grip – impelled me to reject what I saw as its antithesis.

I grew up and my feelings changed, slightly. I still viewed London with suspicion, but without horror. In my final year as a student, I became convinced – justifiably – that all the careers I saw myself cutting a vague but busy stride in, publishing, editing, journalism, had their origins in London life. From the mild confines of my Bristol student flat, I sent out job applications which smacked up sharp against the hectic monitors of offices in Bloomsbury, Goodge Street and Shoreditch, and floated down to join the milling, neutral tide of other twenty-something jobseekers. I was unsuitable for so much: untested, unconnected, proud and shy. I applied to be a Bishops' personal assistant; to manage events commemorating the Holocaust; to run schools' workshops on Shakespeare.

When I finally got accepted for a minor position at less than the living wage, I seized it with desperation. I know my luck, now. I poised the little yellow man on Google maps again over the clotted outer suburbs, and scrutinised the image of myself emerging from what would soon be my local station. I knew nothing about where I ought to live in London, except that, as there was no possibility of being able to do it cheaply – or not what cheap meant to me – it had to at least be non-ruinous.

Robin and I ended up living south-east, just off a long, charmless high street, thick with exhaust fumes, littered with stationery shops and expensive mini-marts and pubs that served cocktails in streaky jam jars. It took a good hour to get anywhere of interest and it was impossible to lure people out to see us, even in summer when the brief charms of the riverside flashed and coquetted in the heat. Our flat was perched above a garage in a retirement complex; by far the seediest thing on that gated estate. The hallway smelt of sour milk and our bedroom wall shimmered with damp for a good eight months of the year that we were there. A porter, there to serve the needs of the official residents, would call, Good morning, with friendly suspicion whenever he caught sight of us.

The toll of spending your time in a stream at once so purposeful and so indifferent is extreme. I found it disconcerting, at first, to wake up knowing that in the same square mile as me, thousands of people were doing the same things: smacking their phone alarms off six times in fifteen minutes, keeping one eye closed in the shower, dumping bread into toasters and smoking under the doorjamb and sponging toothpaste off a cuff. That was just the mornings. Living like this all the time engendered a dumb kind of hardness in me – I spent the days feeling like the phrase *gritting my teeth*. My whole self, from the depression in my chin to the aimless fluff of my soul, felt like one great tooth, grit.

It probably didn't help that I was coming from Bristol, my university city, so gentle, so easy in its texture. There, I'd been able to walk everywhere, to my lectures and classes and between pubs and others' houses, treading the city's stony inclines, which breed a half-jealous familiarity within weeks. And although Bristol had still been the South, still the hazy territory I'd defined myself in opposition to for a decade or more, it still pointed, in its sensibility, firmly away from London. Life in Bristol had been straightforward, even though I lived with two women I found difficult (aspiring barristers on a relentless quest for self-improvement), my classes were interesting enough and I slotted in with an easy group of friends, so that there were people to drink with, dance with, jeer with. Even if the chatter of our group did too often end in relentless sessions of punning, revolving mainly around the names of eminent philosophers, it was still sustaining company to be in. Especially in the winter, when we had maybe five or six hours of real daylight, and I needed a reason to be out of my small and sterile bedroom, while the sounds of competitive partying floated in from the living room. I would stride along Gloucester Road, lit tip of my cigarette glowing through the night, gin astringent in my mouth, and I would feel the warmth of anticipation at the night ahead, no matter how conventional, or underwhelming. That is what my life now has lost, I suppose: anticipation.

Anything after that would have been a shock to the system, and I think my first year in London was a genuinely unhappy one, not marked by any major catastrophe or rupture, but simply by attrition, through an alien dismay. I was not at home there, and though later years reconciled me to London, though at times I found work I liked and ran to a reasonably busy and sometimes genuinely hectic social life, it never struck me as a place to settle.

The friends I had made in Bristol who grew up in London, or Surrey, had a breezy confidence, a smiling lack of interest in our provincial lives that was motivated, I think, more by in-bred conceit than any real contempt. At a work placement in Aldgate, I once asked another intern what he knew about the North and he said, in a pained drawl, that if he was honest, he didn't know *much*. I think part of my own unease in London was defensiveness, too, against what I expected people to think, and say, and care. I was proud of the nothingness, to them, that I came from, and part of my loyalty to that real and imagined space was a refusal to bed down in the capital, and a refusal to be completely impressed.

And now, like most of the places in my life, once left, the impression, no matter how vivid, grows dim and the hold drops within a matter of weeks. After a while it's hard to imagine, I deadpanned to one of Robin's colleagues this week, when we were stranded together at the bar, panning for conversation, that you've ever been any place else.

*

On Saturday evening I joined a table at the bar, and someone said loudly, Making up the weight? I didn't reply, but thought, surely making up the numbers is the correct snub. The weather was bad, and the bar had wheeled heat lamps around the crowded seating area that glowed with real malevolence. I talked with the others there about pets, taxes, the distinct quarters of the city, the people we disliked, the people we had heard things about, and were now dubious about. Later, some of them started high-fiving benevolently. Robin came to sit next to me and held my hand. I like his confidence in this crowd that feels so detached from me, the way he was so at ease, his conversation generous and unforced.

I looked glamorous, I thought, when I went to the toilet, my face sharp and kindly lit, but I felt low, felt like tapping my neighbour's stained tooth, demanding entry, curling up inside with the creamy nerves and enamel.

Robin's colleagues tease me sometimes, when we meet. They talk about long lie-ins, and working in pyjamas. I reply, very serious, and tell them I try to be disciplined but yes, I can't deny the flexibility (they prefer the word flexibility to freedom, and so do I) that a freelance lifestyle like this brings. One of them told me, when I first met her, that she wanted to set up her own company one day: something about books for children, or maybe second-hand clothes; I can't remember. When I asked her about it again, at a recent gathering, she laughed and told me she must have had a lot to drink, that first night we'd met.

*

It's a small, private pleasure to leave the house, alone, on a cold morning and light up. Cool, companionable stick. I chew gum relentlessly afterwards, which is a pain because it becomes weak and tasteless, woolly and good for nothing after just a few hard chomps. It's the smell on the hands that's worse – never have I applied so much hand cream, so much sugary spray, since I started all this again. I remember a friend once telling me about the women in her office, each with her own particular brand of moisturiser in her desk drawer, the greasy reek of citrus, peppercorns and rose. The cruelty of us when we were younger, how we luxuriated in our lack of solidarity, without knowing that was what it was. And how easy it is to cultivate the habit of disdain, a tool for making everything hollow.

Part of that treacherous habit: there's a group I joined online, called 'Ladies Abroad'. I can only ever hear 'ladies' pronounced in a coy, hectoring tone, that close-the-doors-join-the-party clubbiness, I like your earrings and Ooh rosé, lovely, why not make it a bottle? It makes my unsisterly teeth itch. The group is mostly a series of small-business advertisements – waxing, hairdressing, candle-making, street-dance, Iyengar yoga, meditation and actualisation, teas and juices and photo frames and beads strung on bits of wire and thumb-rings winkled out from swatches of felt. And why shouldn't it be that way, I tell myself, why shouldn't anyone choose whatever kind of enterprise they want. I am chiding, self-censorious. There are also pleas for recommendations, for the things the women, or their children, or their partners need or want. Occasionally someone pops up asking if anyone would like to meet, hang out. They always start, 'I am a friendly, curious, twenty-or-thirty-something girl, looking to meet like-minded people…'

*

Work this week has again been long, spewing chains of emails, documents flipped back and forth with creeping tides of annotations, deadlines almost missed. I find it strange, sometimes, to think that these preoccupations are meant to structure my existence, give purpose to my day, be the point of my life. And in fairness, I can't think what I would do with my time if I wasn't doing this. When I worked in an office, I was often struck with longing, on the slow, nauseous bus journey into work, not to commute, not to be a commuter.

Well, I've lost all that now, and still things seem no different. I'm hedged in to working hours and screen-staring by that conditioning, when I believed it didn't sucker me, that I wouldn't be cowed by it. You're never really working for yourself, I think darkly. I mooch around the apartment, picking up objects, examining the rims of glasses. I can't displace the dullness; it's a slow, infuriating itch. I want to talk to someone, I want to have an aimless, comfortable conversation. I send off chirpy messages to a handful of friends back in London. I send a picture of the beach, visited last weekend, a broad flat vista of sea-licked sand, white sky. I cup my hands and breathe into them, taste the faintly meaty fug of my own breath. I go back to work.

*

I'm trying to join in, to catch at the fringes of things. I went to the theatre last night with some of Robin's colleagues: open-air Shakespeare, the stage on the edge of a small and muddy lake, miles from any bus stop. The director spent twenty minutes first explaining to the audience the plots and subplots of *The Taming of the Shrew*. In the programme, next to all the characters' names, they had clumsily rearranged the real names of the actors for comic purpose: Nancy Fly-by-Night; Will E. Norm. That was a misstep, I told myself, and it shouldn't put me off.

This weekend, I tried a choir rehearsal. I'd found mentions of the group online, knew that it rehearsed for two hours on Sunday evenings, in a community centre half an hour's walk away. I arrived to find about fifteen people standing in a pensive semicircle and was handed song sheets with incomprehensible notation, blocks of primary colour half obscuring the words. The choir leader, Joel, was fussy and ineffectual, though he did sway endearingly to our chilly closing rendition of 'Time after Time'.

I had shyly identified myself as an alto, was looked up and down, took off my jumper and told, nonsense, I was a soprano, and sent to stand with three other women. The third woman in my section, Colette, said she was from New Zealand, and also new to the choir. She hectored Joel throughout the evening in a jaunty, bullying way. I could see the other members of the group – who murmured together over coffee during the break, and eyed the two of us blankly – disliked her interruptions. I was dismayed when, at the end of the rehearsal (I had half promised Joel to attend again), she marshalled us into a determined quartet, with the bumptious intention of seeing us all safe home.

The two other women melted sensibly into the hood of a tram stop within a few minutes, claiming fatigue. This left Colette and me to walk the half hour home alone – at least for me it was a half-hour walk. She was curiously evasive when I asked her whereabouts she lived, claiming variously to have had a disastrous accommodation experience; to be living with seven other girls and two puppies in a semi-commune; to have put down a deposit, sight unseen, on a terraced house near the market hall, only to have it all fall through at the last minute.

She told me that, anyway, she wouldn't be here long – her mother was senile and dying, and she would spend most of the winter in Auckland, tending to her. She volunteered that she had had six close family members die on her in the past twelve months and that she would spend most of the autumn in Prague, looking after her cousin, who had recently had a breakdown. My rote, tepid exclamations of dismay and sympathy were ignored, or rather unheard in the determined, bright sphere of conversation she gusted up between us.

When we first started walking, I mentioned that I had come to the rehearsal through the woods, but now that it was dark would perhaps choose a better-lit route home. Colette turned to me sharply, and hissed stagily that I was wise, I absolutely was, because she had heard, in the last week alone, of six girls, all of whom had encountered some funny business walking home on their own, even on the well-lit streets. I made some neutral comment about always needing to be aware of your surroundings, and after a few more moments of silence, she told me abruptly that one of these men had come up to a girl and tried to take her earring – just one. Because it was shiny, she explained, they see it and think – hey, shiny! Maybe I can sell it. It was such a grotesque detail, told to me almost lasciviously in the dark street where I could feel her eyes turn to my own silver studs, that my mind went cold towards her. I resented the ten or so minutes we had left to walk, resented her bristling presence, her blowsy self-deprecation (Now I know they won't look at *me*! Not since I put on all this weight!), which I pointedly made no attempt to deflate.

I felt my dislike for her must be palpable, seeping from my hunched shoulders like gas, but her chatter continued, as did her attempts to draw me out. Had I been here long? I had mentioned a partner – now what did that mean? Was partner a hubby? No one had ever used that word to me before, and my recoil was automatic.

So, I had come here against my will? she continued. Oh, no? She herself had first come here a year ago, but an emergency – something her family appeared to be practised at – had kept her away for nearly another year. She had had a job lined up, she told me, but the delay had knocked that out of the picture, and she was starting from scratch. I almost asked what job, what kind of work she was looking for, but distaste held me back. I imagined idly what kind of work a woman like her would do; I could see her as an officious sub-manager in a bloated HR team, or perhaps some consultant, with an eye-watering daily rate and a different trouser suit for each day of the week.

She questioned me closely about my accommodation, building to an uncomfortable pitch as we came within a few streets of where I lived. She asked what we had paid for our deposit, who had helped us to find it, how it had been decorated when we moved in. I mentioned carelessly that we had struggled to find a furnished place to rent, and she contradicted me calmly and completely: No, I don't think that's true at all.

She revealed that she had actually looked at a few rooms on my street, before her first, forced trip back to New Zealand. She had a curiously insidious way of talking, as though she knew about where I lived and how I was living better than I did. Your place is just down here on the right, she claimed – we were actually two streets away, and had to make a left turn. Well, you can go that way too, of course, she said, casual against my correction.

When she actually walked me to my front door, I realised that she perhaps expected me to invite her up; she lingered for several minutes, talking inconsequentially about the weather. Our meeting eventually ended with Colette taking out her phone and demanding my number, which I offered up with a show of gladness, as if we could pretend this was a gently burgeoning friendship. When at last she banished herself to catch her own tram, I felt an overwhelming unease at the thought that she now knew, down to the gilt lion-head doorknocker detail, exactly where I lived.

Winter

My mind is snagging on the drearier details: how often do others wash their pyjama trousers, their make-up brushes? How do they feel on four hours sleep, or on ten? How often do they look at themselves in the mirror? How do they draw up their shopping lists? Being alone so much, my own habits start to feel normal, and then righteous; I have to remind myself that any other person might look on aghast at this routine.

The smallest things have become sources of disquiet. Last night I lay awake, turning over and over in my mind the furious injunction to chop two onions for the casserole I planned to make on Thursday evening. I could see the white onion scales tumbling ceaselessly into the casserole dish, with its jaunty fringe of painted herbs, but my mind couldn't leave them there, could not even move on to the dicing of the carrots, or turning the lid of the great jar of brown beans. I wasted sleep like this, and spent this morning headachy, irritable, without the freedom to indulge it. Sleep is an uneasy thing for me, almost taboo. I'm too afraid of losing it for good, or even sinking into that low-purple swamp of patchy insomnia, itchy-eyed days. For some years I've taken a medicine, iridescent green syrup in a squat tumbler, which, with the right dose, has me toppling into sleep within half an hour – but too often leaves me dull and thick-headed in the morning. I've played with the dose: drunk too little and lain alert and fuming, or trying a slosh more and then waking in a bright, empty room, the morning gone and useless.

I went to try and replenish this stuff at a nearby pharmacy, a shop called Apothecary, which makes me think of pewter dishes, great pestles and mortars, scales heaped with powdered emeralds and desiccated snake skins. This one was much more prosaic, white and competitively clean. The assistant, instantly dismissing my stumbling explanation in Dutch, told me I could get nothing without a prescription, and instead recommended something herbal. I'll have to look into getting it online: I take it almost every night now, and don't have the mettle to forgo it. I picture the daily dose dyeing some soft inner gland its venomous, bug's wing green. What would I see, if I could see inside myself? Exactly what I'd expect to find.

*

Colette from the choir has my number now, of course. That was a mistake; I realised it almost immediately, that was a big mistake. The first message from her came through the morning after the rehearsal, cheerful, breezy, telling me she looked forward to seeing me again at choir next week. I didn't respond, but she'd have seen I'd received it. A few hours later, I had another ping – she wanted to remind me that she's on the lookout for a new place to live. Could I let her know if I hear of anything? Could I perhaps make a few enquiries, on her behalf, among my friends? And hubby's friends, she added. I waited until evening to reply, and told her that I'd keep an ear out for her. The message was clipped, but she responded almost immediately with a row of smiling faces. What are you doing this weekend? I left the message unread, and took my phone upstairs, so I didn't have to look at it. I had that unpleasant, lurking feeling you always get with a task you're ignoring, something that has to be addressed.

I tried to speak to Robin about her. She's unsettling, I said, there's something unwholesome about it all. He replied that she sounded lonely, and no wonder she came across as intense. He reminded me of a friend of ours, whom I initially disliked on account of his intensity, and told me that, like Caleb, Colette may actually turn out to be someone I get on with. I mentioned the requests she had made of me, how they seemed pressing, pushy, when I was someone she'd only just met. He reminded me about the high rents, the stratospheric house prices, in this city. It's a ball ache, house-hunting, he said. You know that. Maybe the anxiety is making her come across a bit weird. Maybe, I said. I was half ashamed at the strength of my distaste for this woman, my lack of empathy for the practical problems Robin had pointed out. Later, when I went upstairs, I typed out a mollifying reply to Colette. I left it unsent.

*

I've lounged, nursing an anticipated cold, most of the weekend. Now the tip of my nose is starting to scab so I have to constantly smooth Vaseline into it; my desk and bed are littered with crumpled tissues. Yesterday I didn't leave the house. I think the cold may have originated in my trip to the swimming pool, which I was so pleased about just after the act – taking exercise, negotiating another piece of foreign administration. I went in the middle of the day and the pool was full of older people, most swimming sedately up and down, with a few speedy splashy men showing off. I did my fifteen lengths (I'm building up), sticking mostly to breaststroke, which I love – the elegant glide under the water at full length, the beautiful diamond of legs concertina-ing up and down the pool. It was a successful trip, apart from the subsequent cold, and the moment I opened an unfamiliar door, thinking it may lead to lockers, to encounter a very pale, male behind.

Despite the cold, I joined a group of Robin's colleagues for ice-skating this evening. It was someone's birthday. Only a few people actually skated; I lingered by the rink, drinking too-sugary mulled wine, and watching Robin edge and falter his way around the ice while the people I was with talked about end-of-quarter bonuses. One man in a green cagoule kept attempting pirouettes and bursts of backward speed-skating. On the other side of the rink, a kind of target range had been set up, where competitors were throwing small silver kettles, to the accompanying cheers of the crowd. The kettle lids came flying off, skidding along the unbrushed ice every few seconds, while one man officiously kept score on a dingy whiteboard at the side of the arena. I was sorry to leave; I felt as if the winner would surely be crowned with an oversized kettle lid, in suitable style.

*

There are always expensive cars parked on our street, BMWs and Mercedes. There is always a suited man sitting in the driver's seat, reading a newspaper. I wonder if this means there are some significant people living on our street – a few diplomats or politicians. It makes me feel inferior, as I pass the shining paintwork with my bulging fabric shopper full of tinned soup and eco spray. The shapes of the tins are quite visible through the bag. I think of the cautiously friendly overtures of Suzanne, a while ago now, and wonder if she is one of the well-heeled neighbours Perhaps her invitation for a cup of tea, a glass of wine, was in fact code, to which I failed to respond in kind. If there really are people who demand this level of security living on this street, it strikes me that we will already have been subjected to background checks. They'll know everything about us – whatever there is to know.

*

Flakes of snow, unexpected, are covering the rooftops and the gutters. They fill the windowsill, with the same blurring effect that an acid would have – but here it's miraculous, not corrosive. Pigeons butt at the white surface, uncomprehending; dogs in the street below are delirious. The man in the window bay opposite watches, hands behind his back, face impassive. In the evening light the flakes are as dark as ash, and they hurry as footsteps do – I don't like to disrupt them, to be the source of final collapse for a few hundred flakes, smothered against the wool of my hat, gloves and coat. Bikes pass with difficulty, people walk in pairs, shrieking and clutching hands, oddly unseasonal umbrellas held aloft.

*

If I could speak the language better, if I could hold a conversation in more than just a few stilted phrases, maybe I would speak to people beyond Robin's colleagues, beyond the English-language network in which we're so easily enmeshed. I'm finding it's boringly true what they say, that you need to be a child to really learn a language, to let a distinctive tone and syntax seep into the mind's linguistic infrastructures. I learn perhaps ten new words of vocabulary a day – easy things, like days of the week, colours, domestic animals – and find they all slide frictionlessly through my brain from one evening the next. The novelty of going to a Dutch language class, having a textbook and jotting pat little answers to its exercises hasn't quite worn off, although my copy is borrowed from the library, and I have guiltily defaced it in pencil.

I didn't expect it to be my strong point: though I did enjoy languages at school, liked, as I do now, making busy lists of German vocabulary to learn by heart. I only came face to face with a real German person (beyond my teacher, who had lived in England since she was nineteen, an age at which she wistfully entreated us not to marry) on the school exchange, held at the beginning of the Christmas holidays. My exchange partner was a lugubrious girl called Lilli; in the emails we exchanged she described herself as 'the hippo', and in person she moved with a slow, natural grace. We discovered a mutual liking for Heath Ledger, and spent most of the trip watching music videos and film clips in her red-tinted basement. I remember little else of what we did, save for an underwhelming trip across the border into Flensburg, where we spent an afternoon with Lilli's mother bulk-buying towels and tealights. We spoke, at all times, in English.

I think of what the lack of language does to us: an inability to conceive of life in a different register to the one we've been practising in all our lives. There is something so cold, so mean and dull and benighted about knowing no other tongue. It makes me ashamed. It makes me shrink at the lack of generosity it implies, the clipped, complacent edges of my English spirit. It's not always just the Dutch words I fail to find. When I'm talking to people now, when I'm with Robin and his colleagues, or 'our' friends, as we call them now, I find my conversation almost comes vac-packed: I'm reduced to the outline of myself, small and compact, and barely able to elaborate on the facts that were established when we first met. I want to ask people what they're reading, but when I do they tell me, exhaling sadly, that they never find the time. I want to ask if they ever, like

I do, feel like their minds are against them: if they're ever trying to concentrate on a task but are interrupted by pointless demands: unpack the suitcase, clean the dresser, check the clothes are drying, check them again, clean the laptop screen, clean your glasses, check the clothes again, whether this has got worse since they got here, as well? When I have sat, smiling in silence, for too long, Robin always comes and finds me, and takes my hand.

*

Colette surprised me this afternoon. She appeared at the end of our street, just as I was rounding the corner, on my way to the swimming pool. I passed the tote bag containing my towel and costume from hand to hand in my unease. Again, she was clearly disposed to chat, leaning heavily against the dust-streaked window of a bar, her arms folded negligently. She asked me what I was up to, how I had been. She was immaculately made up, the effect of which was to make her seem like an entirely different person to the woman I'd met at the rehearsal: her skin was creamy with what must have been an expensive foundation, a careful wing-flick of kohl at each eyelid, her lips plum-coloured, matte. A waft of jasmine scent came from her as she unfolded her arms, and her hair was teased up, artfully, held in place with two pearl-headed pins.

You look nice, I said, tamely. Are you going somewhere? She ignored me and poked the outside of my tote bag, detecting a purposeful bulge. She asked about the swimming pool, how far away it was, how often I went. I told her what had happened last time, my surprising a man undressing, unaware, and she tsked pruriently. These people take their clothes off at the drop of hat, she said unreasonably.

He was undressing, I pointed out. I walked in on him.

I was at the beach the other day, she continued, and people were letting their kids wander around naked, I mean, completely naked, just everywhere. In the queue for fries, in the toilets. Rubbing their little bellies, showing off. It's incredible. It's dangerous.

I cast around for a new topic. I asked again where she was off to, I mentioned that I liked her hairstyle. She told me, deliberately vague, that she was giving a presentation, and then made a pantomime of looking at her watch, at her phone. Speaking of which, she said, I have to run. Before she turned away, she said, This is your street, right? I nodded and she said, Uh huh. I remember it. How about that. As she crossed the street, she called out to me, gesturing at the window we had both been standing in front of, By the way, that bar is a shithole. My god! A real dive.

*

Monika, from the choir rehearsal, one of the women who resisted walking home with us last week, sent me a message on Facebook today – she must have painstakingly searched for my profile – to say that she had now blocked Colette, and advised me to do the same. Colette, she said, had been sending her passive-aggressive messages late at night, and she wanted to tell me, in case Colette also had my number.

I told Robin about this, and he said, Fucking hell, how mad. I reminded him that a few days ago he was counselling me to be patient with Colette's intensity, to think of her practical troubles. I didn't tell him that I had bumped into her again, the other day, and that I'd found the encounter unsettling but not off-putting, like a faint bruise that's almost pleasurable to probe.

But, he said, if she's harassing people. Is she harassing you? I told him she wasn't, which was true. I felt vaguely put out. I never replied to her message about what I was doing at the weekend; I typed it out, but never sent it. I've left her number unblocked, despite the warning. I have half-heartedly been looking for another choir to join, but I can't pinpoint one that is as conveniently close, and free to attend. I hope, Robin said to me severely, this isn't going to put you off doing stuff.

*

Dentist's appointment today. He had a disconcerting habit of talking over me, even when I was responding to a question he had just asked, and then cocking his head and saying, Pardon?

Before I left his chair, he asked me where I lived, which areas of the city I liked to shop in, if I had been to such-and-such a butcher, a grocer. He talked passionately for some moments about the quality of the mushrooms – to be bought by the handful – in a certain market just a few streets from his house. I mentioned that I had been to the Municipal Market, long alleys of stalls selling baklava, olives, carnations, poultry, trainers, spices and leggings – and he hmmmed, and said with a slight moue of distaste, That is very diverse, I think.

The dentist told me my teeth were stained at the back – tidemarks of coffee, tea, red wine. Very common, he told me, in someone your age. He warned me, too, about fizzy drinks and I told him I rarely touch them, although that's not quite true: I've been stockpiling tonic water, to go with gin, although the tonic is nasty stuff here, flavoured with artificial lime. Gin and tonics remind me of Sunday evenings, meat tensing in the oven, ready to be strewn bloodlessly on waiting plates. The smell of gin and the taste of salted peanuts – which I always ate while waiting for the meal to come to its final pitch – is a combination which now conjures in me an instant, indefinable sadness; something about the wan horror of Sunday nights, the prospect of school in the morning. It's the same when I have a bath (which, as child, only ever happened on Sundays). As I lower myself into the water, I cannot stop that soft inner flood of apprehension, although it has been years, almost a decade, since I had to get up for lessons.

*

I do my face with this or that – expensive, properly creamy stuff for the public-facing days; cheaper muck when it's just me and the house. It's a habit I can't shake, making up my face every day, regardless of who might see me, the same way that I must rise and dress the instant I am awake, no matter how indolent I might be that day. I am losing the sense of my own appearance; it seems, not quite to matter less, but to have less of a bearing on things when I'm not under the quotidian glare of Tube lights, office lights.

Flurries of cosmetic administration seem to rule my life. I so rarely get straight down to work on the meatier tasks, but I dither, fussily emptying my inbox (then emptying my deleted items); looking up bars and restaurants I might visit, making a hypothetical booking for those friends who half indicated they would visit in the spring; reading quickly and frictionlessly through a play text so I can say to Robin, I finished another book today; cleaning my one pair of silver earrings, which now remind me, uneasily, of Colette. It's not just procrastination – these tasks have become something of a doomed web which I must keep spinning to stay creeping anxiety. Every tab on my phone must be closed, but its calendar and notes must be relentlessly checked and updated. These little micro-tasks become circular, never quite cease. Despite their false equivalence, despite how laughable it is to consider the sense of unease these pointless jobs bring with them.

Chunks of each day are spent engrossed in the news, the constant scrolling, the acknowledgement of the tic as I reach for my phone first thing in the morning; as I prompt myself to place the softly glowing screen face down before I sleep. Occasionally Robin or I will declare the bedroom a Device Free Zone, but it never lasts long. One or other of us will ferret the other out, huddled on the toilet, thumb crooked lovingly over the screen. Addicted, even though horrific things stare back at us: people fleeing, people disappearing; diseases borne in the air, and in the water; acts of violence on a catastrophic scale; smaller atrocities in the cities we have lived in that feel even more disquieting for their closeness.

And then another thought will intrude: have we got enough hand soap? Have I checked my online banking for the week? Robin needs to post something to America; I said I would go to the post office. These things stack up behind one another in my mind, a series of open tabs, a jumble of macro- and micro- anxieties. I fret and scramble, thoughts padding aimlessly away from the world my screen is showing me, tumbling gratefully, uselessly from the steel knife-edge of Global News.

*

I'm trying to track my activity here, to keep an anchor on things. For instance, I've started keeping a list of everything I read; I've been doing this since January. In the left-hand column I write the title, the author's name, and the date I finished reading it, and the right-hand column I leave blank for comments or extracts. So far, I have written nothing in the right-hand column, too insistently ambivalent, it seems, for any opinion whatsoever.

I'm remembering the books I liked as a child, when I ploughed, unwholesomely, through whole shelves of jollified schoolgirl fiction. The School by the Low Lake books I remember loving to an almost hysterical pitch. They had been reissued, at the foresight of some canny publisher or other, in the year that I turned seven, and they glowed tantalisingly in their shiny red and blue bindings from across the shop floor. For two or three years, I couldn't get enough of this stuff, with its whiff of jingoism, its hypocritical sententiousness. At least one character was guaranteed to descend into mortal peril every hundred pages or so, and the accidents and misfortunes multiplied calamitously: brain fever, kidnapping, scaldings, car accidents, devastating collapses of ice beneath slipshod feet.

I relished all of this. I can still remember my disappointment when, skipping ahead a few books into the later adult years, I found that the central character, Geraldine, had not succumbed to her mysterious heart illness, as she had been threatening to do across so many instalments but had instead married a physicist and given birth to two sets of identical twins. I was dismayed; I wanted her to be safely dead, tidied away into my mind as the eternal tragic figure that I'd always loved her for. As I got older, I read books with carefully curated references to mobile phones and boyfriends and sleepovers and, occasionally, very heavily censored sex (with dismal results). I liked these as much for the satisfaction of seeing the sequenced titles line up strikingly along my bookshelves as for their on-the-nose content.

I'm reading more, and find that, with little else to occupy my thoughts, the style of whichever author I'm reading starts to inflect them: my inner monologue becomes a pastiche of some other person's way of thinking. So, on some days I pick things up and put them in my bag; I note a message coming in on my phone; I live without affect. Others are florid with detail: the borrowed contempt of a flâneur borne into someone else's mind. I talk myself through the day, occupying the husk of their creation. I like living, at least some of the time, as a person contextualised in somebody else's imagination: I enjoy the romance, the nobility of it.

This glut of reading also means I'm running dangerously low on books. I'm due a visit to the city library, which has a vast selection of English language novels – a much larger collection than the low-ceilinged place I used to visit in London. I once came across a former colleague there, an account director, using the public computers. I asked what he was up to, meaning these days in general, and he told me that he had been trying to find some illustrations to go with the martial arts handbook he had been writing. He'd left, I remembered, under something of a cloud.

The library here, by contrast, is enormous, all whorls and curved edges like a monstrous shell. I come twice a week now; I guard my spot on the third floor, where the students are quieter and the librarians less aggressive. I don't speak to a soul.

*

A call from my friend Jo, back in London, this afternoon jerked me back to something like consciousness: Jo is so much a part of the real, fleshy world. Jo and I met when we were students (she was pursuing a now long-abandoned degree in law); we shared a flat, off and on, for two years, Jo dipping out occasionally to spend six-week stints with a solemn parade of underwhelming boyfriends. Jo's capacity for relationships, for friendships, is prolific. She currently lives in a great crumbling townhouse in Hoxton full of girls who seem to sway hooting and cheering out of every window, eating fruit-studded cheese and drinking extravagantly. When I visited her there, I was left with a feeling of dazzlement, disorientation in the full beam of light Jo casts, and the less flattering gleam it casts on my own life and its dingy corners.

Work is dull, she told me on the phone, sex is the same: she has the ennui which so rarely affects her, and so is felt so much more keenly. She is one of those people who can cry without compunction in public; several times I have stood aghast, eventually passing her a tissue with a wince, as she sobs in an overlit department store, or on a late-night bus.

She has a brother living in America who she is sentimental about, and whenever I speak to her, she seems to be just back from, or just about to dash off on, another transatlantic trip to visit Daniel, who looks excellent in a suit. Daniel is rising through the levels of a New York think-tank like a remorseless, silver-fringed bubble. With me he is always scrupulously polite, with a slightly flirtatious edge.

I told Jo about what I'd been doing, how my work was going, how Robin's work was going. I said I was busy, busy, busy, told her about some of the parties we'd been to, the groups I'd been trying out. I ferreted about for anecdotes, I sketched out a happy coterie of acquaintances, myself and Robin at the centre. I told her about the choir and about Colette. I amplified my own sense of how dismissively weird this was; I made it a vignette about the entitled behaviour you encountered, in this city of expats. Oh my God, said Jo, uninterested, I hope she stays away from you. She asked me if the other people I'd met so far were nice and I told her everyone was very friendly and liked going out a lot. Sounds like a good scene, she said kindly.

I've been thinking about Colette. I still have her number, of course, and she hasn't been pestering me, like the other woman at choir had claimed. I thought back to the rehearsal; perhaps her behaviour wasn't so strange. A bit boisterous, but then it's typical, I thought, to sneer at a woman for her volubility. I thought again, more uneasily, of what she'd said about the men, and the earrings, about girls walking home alone. I can't cast that dislike aside. But what's the worst that would happen if I were to see her again, just for a coffee, just for some casual conversation? If she was still as unpleasant as I remembered, I could ignore her, and based on her silence so far, I shouldn't fear that she'd go on trying to be friends. Maybe a brush-off would be a relief, would stop me dwelling on her. Well? I asked myself. All my brassy self-interrogation shrivelled into sullenness. I'll think about it, I promised myself.

*

I walked past the academy today, saw students sprawled on the concrete steps, or wound about pillars. The boys were all smoking, uniformly shrouded in oversized hoodies and jeans; the girls were more inventive. One passed me wearing a tight white T-shirt, white leather miniskirt, black velveteen waistcoat, the whole thing covered by a kind of poncho of fine black net. A silver pendant hung from her neck and thunked her breastbone delicately with each step. I watched them all, looking so unimpressed and so in control, and thought, drearily, is that part of my life over? I was too anxious, too self-conscious and too furious with everyone else to make the best of it. A forcefully jolly older women once advised me to spend as much time as I could with my clothes off – when she looked back on herself as a girl, she couldn't understand why she hadn't spent more time nude, she was so beautiful.

I don't generally look for advice. In a meeting once, a training workshop, the woman delivering it told us, Your lives are only going to get busier from here. You will never have so much free time again. We were in our early twenties, all women, herded into a windowless room in Blackfriars, and the cramped, sexless atmosphere made me feel schoolgirlish. I couldn't stop complimenting others on their earrings, their plimsolls, their mid-size pleather handbags. When a woman leant over me to pick up a worksheet, I told her how much I liked the jasmine notes of her body spray. At lunch, I piled my plate with a comically large heap of crisps, and smiled at the complicit titters, thrilling to my boldness. The note of stifled hysteria was partly a reaction to the workshop leader. If we were schoolgirls, she could only be our headmistress, with a fussy Victorian frill around the collar of her white blouse, and a pink notebook covered in spangles, complete with fluffy pink pen which she used to jot down our hesitant questions. I don't know for what purpose; these were never answered, or at least not directly. I don't remember, now, what we were there to learn.

Only busier from here, she had said, with the fine, clear contempt of imperfect knowledge.

It's as if Colette knows that I've been thinking about her. This morning, after weeks of silence, a text pinged through: Hello stranger. Do you want to come to the flea market this weekend? Good places for coffee. Bargains!

I waited two hours before replying, and told her yes, I was free on Saturday, after eleven. I'd like to come along. Mentally, I prepared to tell her that I had plans later in the day, so our time together would be circumscribed, heavily if need be.

The outing was strange. I met Colette at the corner of Bakkersstraat, in front of an Italian restaurant. She was staring intently at the menu pasted up inside a glass display case. As I locked my bike and walked over to her, opening my mouth, I felt a squirm of panic. I was uncertain of her attention.

Have you eaten here? she said suddenly. She didn't look up, or make any gesture of greeting. I told her that I hadn't, although I'd had a takeaway from their little booth in the city centre a couple of times, after a night out: Adise Pizza, their sign read, the Par having long since fallen away. I asked her whether she liked it.

She shrugged and puffed out her lips. I can't say, she said, her voice stern. I've never been. She commented on the length of the menu, tapping the display case. I replied, lamely, that I supposed that meant not all the food could be fresh. She ignored me and then stepped back, holding her arms out, as if noticing me for the first time. Long time no see! she said brightly.

We walked back down Bakkersstraat, through the covered stalls of the flea market. I asked her if she'd been back to the choir.

A few times, she said. It's a little slow. The songs are, kind of— not my kind of thing. And they make a big thing about it being an English-speaking choir, but half the time the guy forgets, and he goes on speaking to the Dutchies in Dutch. She shook her head. It's super rude.

I expected her to ask me why I hadn't been back, and felt uncomfortable, and a little pathetic. I hadn't formulated an excuse. But she didn't follow up this opening, instead swooping down on a stall selling mismatched crockery, teacups painted blowsily with flowers, chipped delftware, brown enamel mugs.

Do you like it? Colette proffered a teacup patterned with sprigs of lavender, the gilt around its rim mouthed away in places.

Yes, I lied. I pictured her lips clamped against the china edge, her strong teeth breaking off a chunk. I edged away and bent to look at some postcards of maps, the old-fashioned kind where the edges wobble and blur. Do you know where you are?

We spent another hour like this. I didn't enjoy myself, exactly, but couldn't pretend that I might have spent a more successful afternoon doing anything else. Colette's conversation was an unsettling mix of brassy absolutism and oily self-deprecation. When we queued to buy stroopwafels – hot-pressed, gluey with cinnamon syrup, bigger than our heads – she kept up a constant uneasy chatter about her weight, about how self-conscious she felt exercising, how she felt they kind of shoved it in your face, all the sporty blondies everywhere. Aren't they, though? Asking for it? She didn't say what they were asking for. I felt no urge to ask her any questions, and, as when we first met, I didn't need to: her conversation was incessant, requiring no cues or responses. I was careful, though, to pay attention, and noticed that all the things she had talked about so hectically when we first met now got no mention; nothing of her family, her dying mother, her apartment, her work. Mostly, she complained about the culture here, and how different it was from home, although home was only ever hazily defined.

I made my excuses once we'd eaten, and caught a tram back into the centre of town. She asked me about my plans for later, and I told her that Robin and I were going for dinner, but hadn't decided where yet, which wasn't true. I am disappointed not to have enjoyed the day more. Maybe the lack is in me, a sensation which bores me with its reccurrence. Walking home, I was aware of how briskly I moved, having got out of the habit of matching my pace, pleasurably, to someone else's.

*

Feeling cool, chilled, strung out by the endless dread of cleaning, cooking, shopping, and then real work, paid work, and then anything else – and all the time the significance of these three distinct things bobs and jerks up and down, ceaselessly, so that whatever business I'm at, you can bet I'm simultaneously feeling guilty about that which I'm not. And the smaller anxieties – will I be in time to get the discounted cheese; will I get an answer to my email? – in turn lead on, in a rag-tag, rolling way, to greater agonies. It seems to me that my life at the moment is just one long passage of waiting for either good or bad things to occur, with the bad outweighing the good and far more terrible in my imagination than the small, shadowy parade of possible goods.

I can sit for an hour, clawing at my armpits; I can eke out the composition of faux-casual text messages over an hour. Time dismays me, the thick accrual, the lie of its purpose. Writing to some purpose. I'm sure I've seen that on a mug somewhere. I worry about this, the failure to land. I wanted to live somewhere that brought me satisfaction. If I couldn't find friends here, at least the city itself could have become something close to me, something which offered a kind of binding, a kind of response. The place we live is very handsome, and that's almost all I can find to say; nothing coalesces into any stronger feeling: I can't say, for example, that I hate the alarmist *trrring* the tram makes as it arrives and departs; that I hate the knowing nautical sculptures that flank the bridge by the end of our street. There is no intensity here.

*

It was the final class in my beginners' language course tonight. Some of the students had arranged a dinner for the previous Friday, which I couldn't go to. The tutor treated me unpleasantly for this, as though I'd missed it on purpose. But as I left the class this evening, I could see her steeling herself to say something pleasant to me on the threshold. What cute earrings, she mustered eventually.

The other students were always friendly; Candy and her Latvian-American husband were especially merry and assertive, although with that kind of impermeable cheerfulness that resisted any further intimacy. Candy had never met anyone who had even smoked a cigarette, she told me in a rare burst of candour, before coming to Europe. People were mostly being paid to attend the class by their various employers: they arrived late and left as quickly as they decently could, doggedly chewing through their allotment of HR-decreed hours. I will miss the venue a little, and the expansive health-and-alternative-food shop next door, with its pungent aniseedy atmosphere and impressive range of milk substitutes. It meant we all spent a little more time talking about our relationship to lactose than we otherwise might have.

*

After my failure with Colette – who has lapsed into a silence which frustrates me, though I'm pathetic enough not to break it myself – I think I should again try to find a group of my own, some collective. Something with a nominal structure.

I have previously found this kind of structure only once, in a writing group, in London. There were five or six of us, meeting once a week in an overheated room in Battersea, spaced at intervals around a long conference table. We had no money, but occasionally one of the better-connected people would be able to persuade a guest speaker to join us. One week, for example, we discussed earnestly how to write for a public occasion. Another time a visitor, a pretty successful playwright, asked us if we had ever considered writing with unconventional materials: kitchen roll, say, or lipstick. The group had been set up by a primary school teacher, who brought some of that excessive, laudatory energy with her to our sessions. Everything was beautiful, incredible – which was sometimes difficult to respond to – but then I liked the endless enthusiasm, in the way pessimists can have a reluctant, chilly admiration for unfailingly sunny people.

The stories I wrote in that group all started like this:

'The pig's skin was beginning to bronze and tighten. It was about time, he thought anxiously, napping a little more cider over the flesh. There would be riots if the skin wasn't perfect; he had never seen them, but he had heard the owner, Mr Glebe, speak of them with bitterness. Riots were bad for business, which was mostly bad in any case.'

Or:

'More than old enough to drive, I had failed my test in unspectacular fashion the year before and, until now, had had no interest in a second attempt. Instead, I had looked up the distance from Birmingham to the Devonshire coast where my mother grew up, and found our journey in a hazy diagonal in the bottom left-hand corner of the country, like a careless arm thrown out to gesture to some general possibility.'

Or, my favourite:

'Margaret struggled into the blue woollen dress. It was too small for her and pinched under the arms, but it was clean. Gratefully she felt the cloth between her fingers and drew her nose down to it: no smell of sweat or smoke. Her skin was still stinging. They had used something on her which stung her scalp and made her eyes stream – she knew it was to kill off any lice nesting in there, although no one said as much to her.'

There I usually stopped. I didn't know what would happen next to Margaret, or to anyone else; I didn't much care. Everything I wrote in this vein had someone who was taken in, washed and generously fed. I always got them to the point of physical recovery, and then stopped. And I usually had them in some kind of institution: an orphanage or a hospital – an extension of my convent-bound sleep aid. Margaret was in an orphanage, I suppose. I should have done more research, I thought at the time, for the period detail. But then, I wasn't even particularly sure of the period I was meant to be writing about. Margaret felt Victorian; the turpentine and the cold bath. Perhaps there should have been a lace collar, somewhere.

I had some other things like this, vaguely nineteenth-century, pre-electric light, no water laid on. But sometimes they crept later, into the forties and fifties, reminiscent of the schoolgirl stories I'd read as a child – though I couldn't get the slang right. Wizard, I made my characters say, tentatively. Heavens above.

I can trace the evolution of Margaret. I was fairly solitary when I was younger, and used to indulge in a catalogue of private fictions, all luridly centred on privation. My favourite scenario was to imagine myself as the middle child in an enormous, poverty-stricken Victorian (of course) family, living vaguely 'in a cottage', and even more vaguely 'in the country'. In this world, my mother, broad and cheerful, single-handedly brought up thirteen children, right from the eldest, William (who I usually banished to work in some unspecified role on a neighbouring farm), down to baby Bobby. In some scenarios our father had died, in others he was away looking for work, or even occasionally 'at war'. My own name was Bess, and I was in state of continual poor health. Delicate, as I liked to put it to myself.

Most of my daydreams in this cheerful nineteenth-century world, where poverty chiefly manifested itself in a certain shabbiness of dress and a coarse but plentiful diet of soup and rabbit stew, centred around my battling some commonplace but deadly illness, a cough that threatened to turn consumptive, or an alarming fever brought on by an impromptu soaking in the farm's water butt. At other times, I dwelt foetidly on the family's wardrobe, arraying my six imaginary sisters in gowns (I had got this word from a fictionalised diary of a teenage Elizabeth I, and I hung on to it grimly) of rose cotton or dark green velvet donated by a philanthropic neighbour up at the big house. I liked to imagine Bess in blue, with fine, dark hair and a dead-straight fringe.

In summer, when I ceased for a time to be an ailing Victorian (a fantasy best suited to the colder months), I was busy prowling the woods and forests as an orphan girl, gone wild and returned to nature. I made rapid circuits of my garden, collected stones for mysterious purposes, and assembled dinners of leaves and moss, which I figured into smoked rabbit (even in imagination, my fastidiousness had a firm hold), blackberry cakes and water fresh from the stream. I lived in pelts and travelled once a year to a great gathering of all the wild children, where we sang, danced and, I presume, traded recipes for smoked rabbit. I had a taste for this wilderness life.

When my sister was old enough to be a companion, rather than an annoyance – what a brief window that was – these fantasies lost their grip on me, for a time. One January, Shauna and I decided to each keep a diary for the whole year. I was diligent for about a week, recording tame outings to the cinema and meals of pasta bake. Then I grew bored; I had my entire family killed off by bears (complete with illustrations) on an unfortunate picnic, from which I was thankfully absent. I was sent to live with a cruel, sharp-nosed aunt, but ran away from her at the first beating, and went to live in a forest clearing under the stars. When Shauna and I swapped diaries, a month in, I flicked through her sparse entries, unimpressed: spaghetti dinners, TV programmes, her school timetable. She read mine and then looked at me in confusion, her bottom lip trembling. You killed me! she said.

Temper

*

At drinks on Friday night, I talked to Georgie and Nico, a couple from Anglesey – Georgie is new to Robin's team, Nico some kind of patents lawyer – who arrived late and had no choice but to scrape their chairs over to the gaps at my end of the table. The rest of the group were ripe with chat about the working week, a rash of in-jokes and nicknames flaring. I sat, smiling with pretend indulgence. Nico, taking pity, showed me some pictures of his godchildren, who he clearly adored and spoke of with the shy, self-conscious restraint of habitually reticent men. The children were visiting in a few weeks with their parents, and already he was planning where he would take them, what treats and trips they would enjoy. Georgie then spoke disparagingly, and at length, about Nico's cousin and his girlfriend, who had just announced her pregnancy – She's nineteen, she mouthed, nostrils flaring. I wasn't used to any of Robin's colleagues spending so much time on conversation with me, I was half flattered, half unnerved, and looked discreetly around for Robin, thinking he might give me some cues.

This cousin, the black sheep, Georgie went on, had stolen from them on more than one occasion, small stupid things like gym leggings and an electric pepper mill; he had started an unsuccessful, and illicit, alcohol delivery business; he had once thrown a Sunday lunch platter across the room at his mother; wizened balls of stuffing were still being unearthed years later. Georgie told me all this with mounting distaste, and then sat back in her chair, pulled hard at her drink, and stared with curved mouth at the assortment of bottles and glasses in front of her. It was a slightly performative gesture, for my benefit, but I guessed still authentically felt. I wondered if Nico might chide her on their way home, for revealing so much that was personal to a virtual stranger, but when I glanced at him, he was smiling slightly, and then took her hand. The story told, Georgie seemed to brighten slightly. She asked Nico to fetch her another drink, then, when he left us, apologised to me briefly and said actually, she would go to the bar as well, she wanted to see for herself what they had on draught. I looked at my phone for a few minutes, smiling fixedly, then went to find Robin.

*

It's colder here now, and the quaint old-fashionedness of our flat is revealing itself more and more in its steady draughts and patches of chill. Standing in the bathroom in the morning, my breath hangs in the air, and I frequently fetch down a dressing gown to swag about my legs while I sit at my desk. It reminds me of being a student, when I went to bed a good six months of the year cocooned in pyjamas, jumper, dressing gown and ski socks, with a hot-water bottle slipped somewhere among the layers, like a good luck charm.

It froze – really froze – when Jo and I were in Madrid last year. It was late March and spring should have been hovering, but instead we got snow, sleet and hail, sending us half-heartedly jogging for shelter through the deserted streets. We were there visiting Li, another friend from university, who worked in an office on the outskirts of the city. She lived in quite a grand suburb, though in a small flat that was crammed, like ours, with the landlord's furniture.

We went for two days, drinking vermouth and sangria, eating bread and purplish olives; we lurked for hours in a particular café, known for its cheapness, the floor awash with gritty snowmelt, slipping leaves of cured ham into our mouths and talking of how we would do this again next year. In the metro stations, great gobs of dampened paint hung down from the walls and ceilings in sludgy rags. We were advised not to touch the handrails; people were known to have caught scabies from doing so. I felt less and less that I was at the sleek heart of Europe; the coarse wind, thick with more sleet, blew through and through me, dizzy as I was with lack of sleep. I didn't speak much; I rested my head ostentatiously in my hands when we sat on a bench to consult Li's guidebook. Going to the toilet during lunch at a cramped casa de comidas in the Jewish quarter, I was surprised to hear the voices of my two friends, very distinctly – some quirk of the place's acoustics making it seem as though they were speaking straight through the door. Do you think she's OK? I think she's OK.

*

Walking home yesterday, I saw Colette, who had maintained a radio silence with me, sitting in the window of a café. She was with another woman, someone I recognised, though it took me a moment to place her. It was one of the women from choir; not the one who had subsequently warned me about Colette's messages, but the other. Patrizia, I remembered, was her name. I stood outside the butcher's, which faced into the café, and watched them for a moment. Colette was talking animatedly, Patrizia watching her with a half-smile, nodding encouragement every so often. I walked past their window, looking at my phone, so they'd know, if they saw me, that I didn't see them. I then paused and walked back the other way, passing their window again, still with my phone in my hand. I paused again at the entrance to the café, and drafted a message to Robin. I could still see them from this position, and glanced up to check whether they had noticed me, whether there was any reaction. Colette was still talking; I could just see the hanging edge of

Patrizia's hair, moving as she responded. I deleted the message to Robin and walked away.

*

Last night, when I was in bed, there was a loud shout from the street below. It instantly pierced the thickening membrane of my sleep, like a needle pricking through an eggshell to let the warm jelly slither away. I lay awake for a while, trapped in the scenes of the novel I had been reading before bed, seeing myself as a shadowy supporting character. This trick sometimes helps to coax sleep back, but often it becomes a dazed, faintly alarming half-dream, the import of the fictional life sustaining rather than soothing my restlessness. It's a shame this happened last night – it makes today, Friday, my favourite day, gloomy and itchy-eyed.

This morning was predictably grey and wasted. I can't have slept for more than three hours, or must have hovered on the buzzing, shredded border between sleep and waking for most of night. The image of Colette sitting and talking so animatedly to Patrizia recurred drearily behind my eyelids, heightening my restlessness. I was doubly anguished because I had taken my new little pill, full of its gift of magnesium, or melatonin, or whatever. Sleep should, by rights, have been mine. And then that made me drearily anxious that perhaps that medicine, too, had now ceased to work, and there would be more days like this, more grubby, slackened hours that are below pain, but close to some senseless, sisterly pitch.

*

Dinner with Li, who happens to find herself in Amsterdam, on a three-month secondment. This is already the third month. Her apartment has studentish touches – quotes above her desk, a conspicuous ukulele. She's alone here after years of sharing with febrile young women, and claims to be delighted; never before has she been able to leave the toilet door unlocked. We ate stewed squid, in a darkly glamorous sauce, and drank blonde beer. Li has discovered the trick of living, here and everywhere, more or less. It helps that she is here only for a few months: enough time to absorb and to boast, not long enough to feel the slight, cold nausea of dislocation.

Her neighbourhood was bright and, as I arrived in the evening light, intensely charming; I could see why she looked so cheerful, could imagine a host of friends sitting round her pale, plane-wood table, grinning at their good fortune and eating her sweetish asparagus tips. She comes from money, is pleasantly aware of this, and has the kind of parents that others describe as outrageous, and a pair of brothers who I've never heard her speak of unprompted, either because they fail to meet her own high expectations, or because they so far outstrip her that it pays to be furtive about it. As I chattered, I vetted my own conversation for too much or too little excitement. Coming out into the city evening – still early, by our older standards – I had a hopeless, wavering sense that for everyone else, the night was just beginning.

Li had asked me about how working for myself was going, and I repeated my little stock of phrases: so much more time, can work from anywhere, almost any time, the myth of productivity, pointless presenteeism. I said all this, but I am not under any illusion. I know that, partly, this is another way of working myself, ourselves, out of the texture of things. Adrift in the cloud, I feel atomised, smooth and weightless, without home and without consequence. There's less and less to be defined against: no single occupation, town or city, group of people. Even by the things I enjoy. I met someone at a birthday party a year ago who told me that, having recently quit his job, he'd tried to make a list of all the things he actually enjoyed doing, to work out what he should do next, what might bring him pleasure. It's harder than you'd think, he said.

When I try to do the same now, I find that he's right: I can barely fill more than a few lines of my notebook. Reading, I write. Cooking. Going to the cinema and seeing friends, a small voice in my head adds, automatically. I think blankly about what brings me pleasure. We go to museums and galleries, but if I think honestly about what I do, what I feel, when I'm there, I can't conjure any great feelings of excitement. I glide through, reading the captions, and then go to the toilets and press a powder pad carefully to my face, into the hollow where my nostrils meet my cheek. For some people, I know, the objects and pictures call to them, they are entranced – there is always some answering tug.

*

The train home last night was predictably full of drunks, carriage after carriage swaying with beery bodies. The sounds of the intoxicated must be the same across every continent: the bass *woi-oi-oi*, the crude overfamiliarity masquerading (to its originator, at least) as wit. Two men sat next to me, one in a band T-shirt, shots of grey in his dark hair. He kept belching into his hands, as though disguising a cough. He informed the table next to us, unprompted, that he was a biology professor at the local university; they expressed disbelief and hilarity.

Later in the journey he phoned a woman, an apparent friend, and asked her to join him and his companion for a threesome.

His pal hooted nervously. He then told the carriage that she was a slut – did we know the word? – she didn't care who she did it with. One woman opposite smiled tightly and said that she wouldn't call such a woman a slut. He belched again. The carriage filled with the reek of bile, from some unhappiness taking place a few seats down. I had my headphones in and thought, with sour triumph, that if he leered across at me or tried to touch me that I could threaten him with a phone call to the department he had been stupid enough to reveal, along with his last name. If he had been telling the truth – though it would have been an oddly specific lie. I also thought about what I would say if he tried to approach me; I decided on: FUCK OFF YOU FUCKING PIECE OF SHIT FUCK OFF, which has previously done the trick. Now that I don't work late, am not commuting, am so much at home, these incidents become fewer and far between. Cloistered, I think dully, obviously it's better that way.

I sometimes tell Robin about it: the men who follow you, who try to touch you, who say things. I keep a litany of these events in my head; for some people I know, keeping an inventory of such things becomes simply too lengthy, too depressing. Chatting, in the toilets of a pub with a friend, to have a man swing a cubicle door open, gloating at our shock, telling us he wanted to hear us talk more about our knickers. Walking back from work late, and having my face grabbed by a man who laughed, his breath hot and stinking on my forehead, before he released it. Another who snarled up to me on his motorbike when I was walking home one night along the roadside – dutifully avoiding crossing through the park. Take your headphones out, he kept shouting at me. Your dress is too short. You need to be more careful.

That sort of thing, I tell Robin. Once, when we were still quite early in our relationship, he asked me, in a serious voice, whether anything like that – he left 'that' undefined – had ever happened to me. Am I a woman, alive in the word? I said to him, and he was affronted at the casualness, and embarrassed not to have suspected; too embarrassed to want to continue a conversation that I had little heart for myself. It's everywhere, I wanted to tell him. People you know, friends of yours, will have done things like this.

*

Today was some kind of public holiday, a royal fete, which I only discovered when I left the house to run my thin errands (return a library book, buy ground ginger), and found half the city blocked up and bridled with metal barriers at hip-height. I didn't know about this – why didn't I know about this? I should be more familiar by now, I thought uncomfortably, with the habits and traditions here; I should be alert to the festivals, the days of significance.

People in high-vis jackets stood in clusters every few barriers or so, and their more ceremonial counterparts, in braided red surcoats holding bayonets stood on the other side, spaced at pompously frequent intervals. With the pavements and thoroughfares blocked, it took me an hour to reach home again, striding to areas I thought must be beyond the gala bounds, only to turn again and find the sneer of the barricades. Everyone was wearing comedy top hats, sky blue – some inflatable, some velour, most of the children wore cardboard versions – and waving small flags. I saw patriotic cakes and buns, also be-flagged, on display, and hundreds in the crowds were sporting the bright blue splodges of colour. But beyond this, I saw almost nothing: a few shying horses, bad-tempered with the plaiting and rosetting they'd had to endure for the occasion;

several overzealous police motorcyclists parping through the crowds, and finally two or three sleek black Benzes, in which I just glimpsed some elderly women, dressed in silver and blue, leaning back against the leather. I took a picture of the crowds and sent it to Robin – Did you know this was happening today? – and then, flailing about, suddenly disorientated by the lack of people in my life for whom this might be of even passing interest – a shared geography, how my day was going – I sent it to Colette.

*

It doesn't feel as if we've been here for months, it doesn't feel as if the time's flown by. I'm getting weary of my little trundles through the town, the three or four practised routes I have to get me to the supermarket, the library, the station. Things are so much quieter and steadier here than in London – the most you have to look out for is the odd swerving bike, or the clumsy rump of a bin lorry, reversing slowly through the too-narrow streets.

I sometimes play a little game with myself; I pass the window of a well-known deli in the city centre, famous for its giant meatballs, and if there is one, just one, meatball resting on the silver platter, then I go in and buy it. I see how quickly I've scuttled back to routine. I think of all the times I've said to people, You see, I can arrange my time so that I get to do the things I really want to do.

After I've told them this, I usually go into some horror story about office work, to cement my position. All of it's genuine. Most often, I talk about the second job I had, in a marketing department of a health and wellness brand. Really, it was sales: we were all on zero hours contracts, selling branded plastic water bottles and lunchboxes, athleisure and swimsuits. The slogans we used to sell this stuff were childish; sometimes they were cruel. Working there every day – the six months that I was there – I felt like a blotch, like something worse that a bystander in my own life.

I worked in a team of women, and we all hated what we did, and hated each other with a yellow-throbbing all-encompassing hate. I've never felt anything like it. I used to wake up, just brined in rage, full to the filthy brim with it. I'd walk to work almost spitting, snarling, and then in the office, it all poured out; great heaving bilious gouts of contempt. The other girls would have laughed to see me fall down the stairs and squash my essential vertebrae; it would have given us all a good cheering up. We were managed by Emmy, a kind of low-rent wellness guru, who called everyone my darling, or my treasure, though she couldn't have been more than two years older than the oldest of us. She dressed only in black, accessorised with peach-pink lipstick, and occupied the only proper office, with a door that could be closed. The rest of us frothed and seethed on a strip of hot desks, to which we would stake individual claims by leaving them filthy, littered with olds mugs and used tissues, foetid takeaway boxes. Ladies, Emmy once said, emerging from her sanctum to survey the scene, you are better than this. Emmy's lies didn't even convince herself, which was just as well: having assured us all that profits were strong and work guaranteed for another six months, a week later we were all told by email that the company 'had failed to keep pace', and our services, from Monday, would no longer be required. Emmy had been absent that morning, her desk empty, a faint stain on its surface where her tray of miniature succulents had stood.

In my last job, in a dreary market research team which partly inspired my enthusiasm, our enthusiasm, to move here, I used to make my way to work dreaming about what else I could be doing with my day. Not in the usual vein – not having a lie-in and watching morning TV kind of pangs – but an imagined timetable of occupation both glittering and serviceable: matinees to review, bookended by boisterous lunch meetings with critics, actors and producers. Anything but the world to which I really belonged, trailing in and out of meetings, talking always in one of two registers – one in which the obvious was stated, earnestly, and one in which our past, current and future activities were discussed with synthetic heartiness.

Returning home from my tedious cubicle, I had to reassure myself that my great and necessary affectations were not a sign that I was a bad person – just, in this particular sphere, an indifferent one. There never seems to be the time, within the machine of work, to understand whether your indifference, in particular, is symptomatic of an essential malaise, or whether it's simply because you're working, with stiffening joints and reluctant elbows, in the wrong part of the machine entirely.

The last years in London were spent always rushing, always knackered, sick of the truism of the bad-tempered, breakneck city. I used to get off my train at the foot of St Paul's and walk into the East End, into Whitechapel, past poor Queen Anne, past St Mary-le-Bow, the Bank of England, skirting the poisonous glitter of the Gherkin. I took my life, diffidently, in my hands every time I made that journey, because the crossing points were poorly marked and the roads choked with traffic. A bus once came within a hair of me: I was still pavement-bound as it jolted onto the curb, and the man next to me said, a little too cheerfully, We were both just nearly killed. On my lunch breaks, I used to see blue-suited businessmen slumped outside the food courts and coffee shops, smoking small, pungent cigars. They looked like deflating profiteroles; I felt that if you poked them, tobacco-coloured cream would ooze out.

I don't want my mind to run on its own fumes. So much of the conversation here is about what people have done, the trips they went on, the countries they've visited. It's a forest of anecdote, and yet no one in Robin's group of friends and colleagues is much above thirty; I feel too young for this. Or maybe that's defensive, it's more that I know my own anecdotes are so thin in comparison. No one really needs to hear about London, or Bristol, when they can talk about Jakarta, Hong Kong or Manila.

*

On Saturday night eleven of us gathered around a small table in the living room, the TV on in the background to provide a prompt for conversation. Our host, one of Robin's colleagues, even more recently arrived than us, was very sweet. He told us that he let his landlord's brother stay in the spare room from time to time, because he was afraid of rent penalties if he refused. He only smiled when we told him this couldn't be legal. I knew everyone present, apart from one girl who had recently moved to the city, who was chatting to the other women with a familiarity that I had not managed in the months we had been here. When we arrived, she was telling a story about a failed date, and the rudeness of the man she'd been with. He told me, she said, that my education was misaligned with my career. That I had no clear direction. That my skin was bad, and that I shouldn't smoke. The others tsked with collective outrage while I arranged my face to match, trailing a tortilla chip through a plastic tub of hummus.

Later, I asked Robin if he would tell me if my skin was bad. I mean, if you noticed it getting worse, I said. He was cycling us both home, me perched behind him on the carrier. I enjoyed the feeling of detachment I had, riding like this, the relief of my safety being in someone else's hands. I'd never say something like that to you, he said, even if it was true. His voice whipped away from me as we neared the bridge at the end of our street, and I thought of our nervous host, putting every glass and plate back in his cupboards, exactly where he found them.

*

Sometimes I think all anyone wants is to know one place better than anywhere else, to be part of the texture of one location, to be *of* somewhere, not just in it. I want this, very much. It's like the feeling I get when I'm in the countryside, or when I tell people that this is where I like to be. Not just unease, the knowledge that this is not really the place, after all, but helplessness: not here, so then where? I'd like to give somebody else directions, I'd like to have opinions on local matters. A naff bleat. And it's harder to care about things here – the social life, the physicality of the city – because it's so obvious, has been for months, that this is not the place either. And I know this comes from us, something we carry with us, heavy and sharp-edged, for all the hollowness at its centre.

I still check the local news where I grew up, when I remember. The stories are unchanged: a smattering of traffic accidents, petty violence and theft, discontent with the management of local schools, opposition to the proposal of a new Business Improvement District. And then, always, a celebration of a hundredth birthday, or occasionally a husband and wife, or pair of brothers, celebrating some momentous joint anniversary. The photographs that accompany these stories are all the same: an unsmiling, faintly alarmed-looking man or woman, invariably snapped in a pale armchair against a pale background, a card or cake propped unnaturally in their laps.

*

Colette has been in touch again this week. After I'd sent her the picture of the crowds, she sent me one of the teacup she'd bought at the flea market. I thought the subtext was obvious: should we do something like that again? She's started to message every few days, carefully spaced. It's all neutral stuff – pictures of the beach, or a piece of public art, things I can respond to blandly. We had drinks planned for Friday night, with Robin's colleagues, at a bar in town. I toyed with the idea of asking Colette. There was nothing altruistic about this; I was aware that, several months in now, I had failed to generate any real connections, any alternatives to the precarious threads Robin's colleagues offer. But I couldn't forget our first meeting, the sense of deep disquiet she left me with, that weeks of tame text conversation has failed to dissipate – although she hasn't said anything further to solidify that original discomfort. I wondered if I was overly touchy, unused to that strand of intimacy and interest, particularly after those rootless first few months. Giving her a get out, I thought to myself, unhappily. I scanned back through that first encounter: no, I assured myself, it was all there.

I decided to invite Colette to the drinks. She replied asking for detailed instructions on how to find the bar, which puzzled me. It was in one of the main squares, a brightly lit scattering of gin lounges and old-fashioned brown bars, thronged with people.

The bar itself, Oskar's, was large, plush, easy to find, the kind of place that's always crowded at weekends. It had no particular reputation – likely because of its largely English-speaking clientele, me among them, and the predictably antiseptic effect that has on any place we frequent – but it was well known. Although clearly not to Colette.

I told her to meet us at eight. We arrived at half seven, and I drank a beer, quickly, trying to snip the threads of unease unwinding in my gut. Stupid, I told myself severely, to feel like this. The others arrived singly and in pairs; the conversation soon became loud and general. One man, Conor, held sway, talking about the trip to Amsterdam he had planned for the next day, with a girl he's been on a few dates with. Is she Dutch? I asked, and he said, God, no, a Dutch girl wouldn't look twice at me. I'm not fooled by the self-deprecation. Everyone had a faintly smug, at-ease air, the working week done. A tray of breaded snacks arrived and was lazily pushed about. Beer slopped onto the glass-topped table. I checked my phone: eight fifteen, no sign of Colette. I hadn't mentioned to anyone, except for Robin, that I'd invited a friend outside of the standard orbit. Is your mate coming? Robin asked me, and someone else caught it, and asked, Who's this?

Just someone I know, I said. I met her at a thing, she's from New Zealand. She might come along, I'm not sure. And then, cravenly, I told them how Colette hadn't heard of Oskar's, had to ask how to find it – Can you believe it? I said. They hooted complicitly. Where the hell does she go, then? asked Conor. One of the old-man bars? I didn't want this conversation to spike the atmosphere when Colette eventually showed up. I shrugged and made a play of wanting another drink and being unable to decide which. I asked a few of the other women in succession what they were drinking. That looks nice, I repeated, is it nice?

We moved bars and I updated Colette assiduously, faux-casually, each time. She didn't come, of course; each of my messages showed as unread.

I felt slighted. I didn't have sufficient magnetism in the group for my disappointment to be noticed, or even for the fact that I should have had a friend coming to be remembered, after the third round of drinks.

*

Everywhere there are lights, there is singing, the moon glimmering palely in the smoky air like the flesh of a lime. It would be easy, comforting, to dig in, stockpile, take cover and resurface in the new year. I sometimes idle away the dead time while we are staring at the television by imagining how I would act if I knew a siege was imminent. Or if the power went off, for weeks on end. Or if, *Handmaid's Tale*-style, new and terrifying martial law came into place, with curfews enforced and women forbidden to take employment. The first scenarios are easy enough: I am already cautiously proud of our canned goods collection, so it would be a case of getting to the supermarkets, or better yet the wholesalers, quickly and buying economy-sized cans, sacks of rice and grains, kegs of fresh water, in bulk. Remember salt, is my main memento to myself in this hypothetical future; you could subsist for a long enough time on chickpeas and pasta and tinned peas, but salt would take the edge off their monotony. Fuel is trickier – if the gas went, and the electricity, we would have to improvise with layers of clothes, stuff up the cracks in the poorly insulated windows with clumps of wadding. Still, two bodies are better than one, in these kinds of situations.

The third scenario is more difficult. I have several different versions of it, depending on the leniency of the ruling force. Mainly it involves adopting a quiescent domestic demeanour while engaging in deliberately subversive acts – though I can never quite work out whether I'd be bold enough to join, or initiate, an underground resistance network, or simply opt for resistance of the mind. Whatever happens, at some point in the scenario I am stockpiling cash somewhere in the house, skimming off small wads from the household allowance (or whatever) so I can fund my eventual escape. In this scenario, Robin always becomes one of the enemy, even if unwittingly. No one is to be trusted.

*

We've put up our little green tree, our modest assortment of Christmas baubles and decorations, collected mostly from European Cities of Note. The Kölner Dom, masterfully figured in laser-cut wood, glowers down at me from above my desk, while the Sagrada Familia, caught in a hot red hoop, dangles from the kitchen door handle. Cheap white lights fringe the mantelpiece. Outside there are markets, ranged all around the city centre in spiky strips. They sell German biscuits, mulled wine, Christmas tree decorations, candles and soaps. At set intervals, these offerings repeat themselves. The canals run darkly between these various outposts, the stallholders' lights reflected tremulously in the water.

Overexposure to the picturesque is leaving me cold to it. We live beside a canal, the water bisected by a small humped bridge, painted green and strewn with flower baskets. Carnations bloom and brim over into the water, year-round. On one side of the bridge is a small bakery, displaying a yellow painted sign and glazed loaves. Opposite, a café, which in the warmer weather provides chairs and tiny, chrome-topped tables for its patrons to sit at while they sip coffee and eat a sandwich, teeth moving sturdily in the bread. A tidy strip of houses lines each side of the canal, narrow and neat-bricked with dark wooden shutters and red-tiled roofs, their doors all painted to a glossy finish. Bicycles lean negligently against the brick in the spaces between doors. Every few hours a swan will glide through on the water below, or a small pleasure boat will chutter past, its occupants grinning as you watch from the bridge.

Occasionally a portable toilet will appear. A skip will bloom outside one of the neat houses, and purple netting will creep across the windows. Rubbish bags will be left out to split and fester. I might be walking across the bridge and feel something slide under my heel: a piece of orange rind, or a hank of wet wipes, clotted together. Then I feel glad, and I make my way past the café's steaming windows with satisfaction. But then of course – I return at lunchtime and the rubbish is gone. The skip is whisked away on the back of a lorry by a whistling official in a blue uniform, who will also dispose of the portable toilet. The netting comes down and the eyes of the house gleam again, their paint renewed, heightened to a malevolent shine.

You'd think, in my own flat, that I'd cultivate an atmosphere of shabbiness and discord, to combat all this. But I don't. That cheery external aesthetic seeps into you, into your vision and your movements. It's like a slow wasting disease, gradually attacking the centres of taste, so that the cushions are placed just so and meaning I have catastrophically failed to remove the landlady's little red-varnished cabinet, so squat and cheery, so pleased with itself.

Spring

A brief holiday back in London, the memory of which has already vanished, bitten off by the limbo that comes towards the end of February, when I stop straining towards the new year's purpose and admit failure. I'm still holding on to the sense of freshness I had, coming back: the plane coming in to land over the network of waterways, the wrinkly skin on this bowl of cosmic soup.

While we were in London, I managed to see my sister briefly, along with her boyfriend, who talked breathlessly to Robin about the Champions League. Shauna talked about her job, about the Christmas parties she'd been to. At one event they'd had a giant inflatable stiletto, filled with pearl-pink balloons: she showed me pictures of herself lying in it with a crowd of other women, all glossily attractive, all dressed in black. She scrolled rapidly through half a dozen of the badly lit photos on her phone. That's Alix, she pointed out, that's Celeste. I squinted politely. How fun, I said lamely. I told her about the Christmas party we'd held at our flat, half of Robin's office in attendance, the half-ironic playlist Robin had put together, Shakin' Stevens on blurry repeat while I mixed cranberry juice with a litre bottle of white wine in our kitchen, the windows opaque with people's breath. Wow, said Shauna, her eyes still on her screen, that sounds exciting.

I had asked her if she wanted to come back over with us for a few days, see the flat. We could go into Amsterdam, I offered, I can show you some of the places we've found. There's a really fun speakeasy, not far from Central Station. Shauna told me she couldn't, work was too busy at the moment. But she hoped they could come in the summer, her and her boyfriend. A badly timed transfer, I could hear him murmuring to Robin, it's obvious to the fans, but the club are having none of it.

*

Recently I've been hooked on mukbang videos: a Korean word and concept. It's people filming themselves eating, and you wouldn't think it would be so addictive, but I'm compelled, over and over, to trawl through the selection of clips, turning the sound down on the slurps. My favourite ones are where the person is eating noodles, or spaghetti, something long and stringy, and dripping in broth or sauce, gobbling them down, a huge portion, a grotesque amount. Why I should get such a kick out of that, I don't know. They don't do much else, the mukbangers, sometimes they give a thumbs up, or dab their mouths with a paper napkin, or comment briefly on what they're eating, whether it's tasty or hot or spicy. The worst videos, the ones I glide right past, are the ones where the person tries to give a little spiel about something totally unrelated, like self-care or seizing the day or whatever, all while they dip seafood into mayonnaise or poke big wads of rice into their cheeks.

I like these videos because they're all brightly lit and cheerful and make you feel alive, probably because eating is a key component of the MRS NERG acronym that we were taught in biology, which summarises the key characteristics of all living things: Move, Respirate, and so on. We studied nutrition, too, in those lessons, as well as diet and exercise. One week for homework we all had to calculate our own BMI and write a paragraph on whether this represented a healthy weight or not. I remember when I calculated my BMI I was slightly, ever so slightly, underweight, being an anaemic sort of teen, and the teacher wrote kindly in my book next to the calculation that I shouldn't worry about this, as no major health concerns were to be expected.

To this day I have no major health concerns, though I have a noticeable chip in my front tooth (caused by, of all things, a piece of chewing gum) and I'm afraid the tooth will one day sheer off completely and leave all my nerve endings exposed, blinking in the raw light of day. And then I sometimes feel dizzy when I'm out. Not after walking particularly far or robustly, just normally out and about; I start to feel slightly light-headed and out of my self, a whisper of nausea passing over me. Then I get anxious in case it means I'm about to collapse in a public place, about to be fetched a glass of water by a solicitous shopper. Sometimes I think this is a side-effect of my sleep medication, which can't, after all this time, be good for me. Recently I've been waking up drenched in sweat, the hair at my temples sopping, the bedsheets wrinkled and wet through. After a couple of nights of this, the sour smell of sweat on the bedding was overwhelming, insistently vinegary. I rolled myself up in the duvet. Look, I said to Robin, I'm a chip.

And now my leg is bothering me. The pain starts in my left calf but rolls up and down – sometimes it squats at the base of my spine, sometimes there is pain – *ping ping* – in my thigh. I would describe it as a dull, persistent ache. I type *dull persistent ache in thigh* into Google and spend half an hour reading about deep vein thrombosis, and the different types of bone cancer. I break the news, in my head, to several different friends and family members.

The imagined results are gratifying. I grow bored of this. At night the ache is worse, and a specific soreness in my throat becomes a new distraction. I get up and silently sit on the toilet, worrying. I think about the smoking – a contributing factor in thrombosis, so I've read. In the darkness, I picture the smoke of the past three months, coiled and deadly in my silent lungs.

In the UK I went to give blood regularly. It was a way, I thought, of ensuring that my life hadn't been wasted, even if nothing happened in it, even if I did nothing very remarkable: I could still have saved someone else's life. Or at least have contributed to medical research, which still felt useful, if not heroic. Here, they won't allow me to donate – something about mad cow disease, some lingering distrust of what might be lurking in the blood cells, or the soft, dreadful circuits of the brain.

When my uncle was dying, my main memory is of becoming absorbed in an online sweetshop. We had a sweetshop in town, but it was one of those tobacco-and-sweeties affairs (like the ones derided in *The Witches* as being poor hunting ground for kids) and the midget gems went stale from one week to the next, and the shopkeeper wasn't above giving out dud change to the shyer kids (I was once marched back to demand a substitute for a Guernsey fifty-pence piece). This one had all the glamour of being virtual, and of stocking almost anything you could want to eat – from Chelsea whoppers, huge oblongs of soft fudge dusted with cocoa, to bubblegum coated in gold dust and bagged appealingly in small hessian sacks. I was on my half-term holidays and as a treat to myself had ordered great pound bags of jellies and chocolate shapes. My memory of that grim week, flecked with hospital visits and urgent adult conversation and a barely lidded irresistible panic, is also bound up with the slightly salty, plastic sweetness of chocolate pigs, the impulsive diarrhoea caused by overconsumption of gelatine.

*

I'm becoming involved with a small theatre here; I offered to do some volunteering. Their offices are based inside a now defunct children's home, for which their company acts as the building guardian, to discourage squatters. We met there this afternoon and sat in a back garden, under the sun. I could feel the skin of my thighs flaming through my tights. I was sent a link to a recording of a recent performance, an ambitious production of *Death of a Salesman*. The women I met with had both watched and re-watched this; they loved and were amazed by it. Particularly, said one, because the main guy – well – he is a little fat guy, right? He is not handsome. Later, one of the women, Nella, told me two things I might like to look up. She asked if she should write them down for me, and when I told her not to worry, I would remember, she looked at me and said, Wow, superbrain. I couldn't tell, and still can't, if she was mocking me.

*

I messaged Colette, cautiously, to ask her if she'd like to come to the theatre with me. I didn't ask myself why I was doing this until the message was sent. She replied to ask what the show was, and didn't respond when I told her. I worked sluggishly through the afternoon, constantly glancing at my phone – its screen remained dim. I went alone, eventually, and afterwards stood talking to a woman I had met at my Dutch language class, Zulema, both of us adopting that tone of arch enthusiasm used by people who don't know each other very well and are keen to appear creative. We talked about language and Zulema revealed that she no longer thinks in Catalan, only English. The only time she reverts to her mother tongue is in her dreams. I said that in my dreams I am sometimes speaking another language, absolutely fluently, although I have no idea what this language is, or what I am saying. I looked around for someone else to talk to; the rest of the audience all seemed to know each other very well.

Later, both trying to leave, we were caught in conversation with Nella, the general manager from the theatre. I repeated my comments about the performance, and Zulema shared some joke with Nella while I looked on blankly and wondered if they had met before, perhaps were neighbours, but no, this was their first meeting. We were introduced to the director of the board who said, menacingly, that she was glad to be able to put faces to names. Hours later, I got a message from Colette: Sorry, she said, I fell asleep.

*

On the nights I can't sleep, I play out one of several scenarios in my head. They are very tame. I have little else in me. My favourite, perhaps because I think it is the most restful, is to visualise myself as a novice in a convent. I picture the room; it is a private room, although in reality I have no idea if nuns are afforded this luxury, or whether they all sleep together in one large room, like a boarding-school dormitory or hospital ward. In my mind, however, I have my own room, stone-walled and cool, with a bolt on the door. I picture a narrow bed with grey blankets and white sheets, a wooden chest that holds my puny possessions, a small washstand with a bowl and jug of water, a chair with a dusty red embedded cushion, which resembles the hassocks I've seen in churches. There is a window, which sometimes is mullioned and sometimes plain. These various details suggest I must be a nineteenth-century nun, perhaps even an eighteenth-century one, but I don't linger on the time frame. Instead, I bring to mind the textures of the room: wood and iron and cloudy glass, coarse wool, the chair's prickly stuff. I lie stretched out in the bed wearing a long white nightdress, with cuffs and a high collar. I am vague about underwear.

There is a rosary, somewhere about, which sometimes has wooden beads and a large, roughly hewn crucifix, and sometimes is made of Whitby jet, the edges of the cross enamelled. I can't always decide where in the room this lies – whether on the washstand or beneath my pillow or coiled in my closed fist. My hair is always very long and blonde, with split ends. I know that it is plaited and hidden in the day, although at night, which is where I always begin, it is loose on the pillow. I have the knowledge that I must be up before six for morning prayer, from which follows the day's regime of praise and contemplation. I think about how the hysteric agony of heightened emotion is pleasurably subdued to timetable.

In my own bed, I match the pace of my breathing to that of the nun-me, gentle and ritualised. I can never work out the depth of her faith, in this fantasy: is she there at her own insistence, or has she been shuttered away against her will, a useless, undesirable daughter? I concentrate again on the physical sensations she apprehends, texture and scent. Her mind is carefully blank, which of course is a symptom of proper discipline. And this puts me to sleep.

When she rises, what does that day look like? I can't get away from the early image of washing in iced-over water at the ewer, although I'm still unwilling to commit to a specific moment in time, a historical period. How clean could you ever get, only ever washing in a basin, in water someone else had probably had first? I imagine a general hum, below the waist. Waves of female stink rising like prayer, probably carefully diverted to some particularly feminine saint. After the ablutions, the hasty dressing in coarse clothes – song? Prayer? Would there be candles, so early? And I can't figure out what the position would be, whether the women are kneeling, or sitting, or standing for their early devotions. Not prostrate, that much I have decided.

I'm on firmer territory with breakfast, which is served in a long white-lit communal dining hall (definite shades of boarding school now), those spindly laminate-topped tables with thin metal legs, the smell of long-warmed cheap fat in the air. I give everybody porridge, tea that is too milky. They can have jam if they like. There is a serving hatch, with two sisters doling out (as decreed by the rota); all help clear at the end of a meal while these two again wash up in a deep, industrial sink. Poking little clots of congealed porridge down the plughole, one sister passing the own-brand bleach. It's not quite a friendly atmosphere; I don't think nuns are supposed to have friends – real friends, as opposed to general benevolence towards everyone. I imagine that their one overwhelming relationship crushes all other tentative sentiment.

If I'm still not asleep, by this point, I picture nun-me returning to her room after breakfast. I have her collect a series of quaint materials – a leather-backed prayer book (what prayer book? Vague again, beyond some idea of a kind of *Book of Hours*), that shape-shifting rosary, a thick notebook and pen. Some kind of library-bound nun, she is, although I think that's an unlikely position for one so young. Otherwise, I sometimes have her chopping vegetables for a communal lunchtime soup – plain root vegetables, leeks and carrots and potatoes. I imagine it very under-seasoned, this soup, and served with unwarmed white batch rolls that always remind me of looming constipation. The novice at study, the novice at work. I don't picture her outside the convent walls, or if I do, it's to tend the garden or the hives, muddling into monastic territory. I don't have her hefting a carrier bag full of tins to a food bank, or talking to children about God, with a fluttery manner and a fixed beam. She is working towards something. She is working out the relation between herself and various metaphysical factors; that is, a proper programme of study. I rarely get this far. I try to fix on the picture of her in her cell, at night, her quiet breathing, her learnt attitude of repose.

*

I've been thinking about loneliness, and how it's portrayed: the dramatic, swingeing aspects of loneliness in the crowd, the abject feelings of people who still contrive to go out and get pissed and get laid and go to work and have demanding social lives and relationships and strong ideas about themselves and other people. Which seems to me to be less about loneliness – even if we do see them, mascara-smeared and anguished at 3am, scrolling through a list of numbers – and more about metropolitan ennui, shackled to anxiety. The loneliness I know more about, or feel an affinity with, is real solitude hitched to everyday dejection, no place to meet other minds, and sometimes no inclination to even do that. It's much more boring to depict, so not coming across it often, people are less sympathetic, or find it a less credible state. Stale, monotonous, not always unpleasurable. But it bites deep, can set a hard-to-shake pattern.

The world belongs to us, too – the soured, the aimless, the chronically unenthused. Sometimes I feel like this; the larger disgruntlement at how there is a whole dismal narrative underlying everything, of people who don't feel excited or interested, or ambitious, or purposeful; that if you raise any of this you get shouted down as a cynic, how the white teeth of positive power gnash you back, with your tired world view, your lack of contentment. But so many millions go uncontented to their deaths – and it feels as if that is never acknowledged. In some lives, nothing ever happens, and nothing may change for the better. We can't celebrate it, but— be quiet about it? I would still advocate for the significance of the soured mentality, in any serious discussion.

I've been thinking about all of this often: when I was eating chips with Robin at the beach, when I was talking to his colleagues at somebody's birthday party, when I was trying to escape a conversation about high taxation that followed the cutting of the cake. I can see the allure of simply dismissing it all, holding it all at a careful distance, reducing the contact. I suppose the answer is in the proportioning of pain, of the risk of pain, to the pleasure, and that there is a calculation here, and probably one path is not, in the main, a great deal different from the other. I think of my friend who won't leave England, because he's content with what he has in this blue-fringed cell, and won't run the risk of anywhere else being worse. Is he so much unhappier than anyone else? Probably not. These are despondent arguments; I don't like myself for making them. If they were raised in the pub, I would defend the opposite view, the empathetic view, the wide horizon.

What is the engine of your contempt? I ask myself this, over and over, the thrum of it sitting behind every bland action, every wizened thought.

*

Yesterday, Colette and I spent the evening together. She asked me if I felt like doing something on a Friday evening, and suggested a bar a little outside the city centre, which was famous for its hot wings challenge – if you could eat a whole basket without taking a drink, you got a free round. I dressed in a casual outfit, which I had tried on the day before. I applied lipstick and blotted it with a square of tissue, which I threw into the toilet. My red Cupid's bow smiled back at me, blurrily, when I went to flush. This is something I might often do, I told myself, a drink with someone I'm getting to know.

When we met, I jokingly asked if she planned for us to try the wings challenge. Fuck that shit, she said instantly, it's always such sad guys that try and go for these challenges, you know the ones: wearing branded T-shirts, their guts sticking out. Then they throw up all over themselves. I told her about my mild obsession with mukbang, and she asked if they kept their clothes on in the videos. I told her they did, or at least in the ones I watched. Some kink, she said.

I asked her what she wanted to drink. She ordered vodka and Coke, and asked if they could bring any olives, or peanuts. The barman addressed us initially in Dutch, and where I might have cravenly attempted to make the drinks order, at least, in the same language, she ignored this and replied loudly in English. As soon as we found a table, I realised I didn't know what to talk to Colette about. The choir seemed a non-starter; it brought back to me my guilt at failing to attend another session. Colette seemed unfazed by the awkwardness of the moment; she shifted on her stool and stared around her, smiling slightly. Her whole face seemed to be drawn into the curve of that smile, while her eyes were busy calculating, assessing the other drinkers, moving in every direction apart from my own. I grinned awkwardly, and eventually launched into a story about the theatre group, assuming that Colette would pick up this thread, considering the invitation I had made the other week, and her failure to respond. You fell asleep, I reminded her, I thought maybe you'd like to see something. I could let you know again, when something else is on.

Colette didn't reply to this directly, but instead told me that her brother had once been a props manager, and almost got sued when some fake blood had resulted in the permanent blindness, in one eye, of a cast member. They were only students, though, she said, so it didn't go anywhere, thank God. She told me that she'd been a box office assistant at a large theatre when she was a student, and once found a death threat pinned beneath her desk, written on an old ticket. The police had to come and do handwriting samples, she told me. That was wild. She changed tack and started talking about her trips to the beach here, how much she liked windsurfing, how it reminded her of the surfing at home. I asked about her mother.

Living her best life, Colette told me. She's moved to Whakatane now, she's soaking up the sun, the sea. She never wants to leave. And if I were her, neither would I. But things aren't easy for me there. I ignored this and asked, cautiously, But wasn't she ill? Like, very ill? Didn't you have to go and see her?

Colette said, My mother's never ill. She's got that ancient hippy thing going for her, she'll live forever. She'll only die when the moon goes out.

I wondered what would happen if I said, then: So it wasn't true then, what you told me, the night we first met. I left this unsaid, not out of embarrassment, but more a sense of what a redundant question it would be. I knew Colette was lying, had been lying constantly and casually whenever we met, without thought of reproach. And really, when I considered it, I had no reproach to make. Why shouldn't I be lied to? What did it matter to Colette, what did it matter to me, if the things she said to me had no representations in the real, hard practical world? I was lying to Colette as well, by coming along with her to a bar, by inviting her to the theatre, and out with my friends, by nodding at her conversation and promising to watch her bag when she went to the toilet: I was pretending to be a friend. I'm only curious, I thought, as I ordered another glass of wine, and another vodka for Colette. I only want to spend some of my time, and this is as good an exchange as any.

When she came back, I told her I liked the bar she'd chosen, and that I was sorry she hadn't been able to come the last time I'd invited her, to Oskar's.

Oh? She mimed trying to remember, her eyes flashing upwards. Oh, right. Well, I had a friend in town, and I told him about the plan, and he said he didn't want to be in any of the bars near the Plein. Too busy, he's kind of agoraphobic. Worried about bombs. But next time, I'll come. If my friend's not in town. She laughed derisively, as if at some private joke, but didn't explain it. I wondered if she and the guy were seeing each other, but then reminded myself that in all probability, this man did not exist.

Throughout the evening, her responses were brusque, unapologetic. There was no amiable discursiveness to Colette on this occasion; even when she was telling an anecdote, its intention was to counter some point I was making, or to pointedly enhance the theme I had begun. Her conversation was executive, I thought, half admiring, as she grated the olive flesh from the stone with regular sawing motions of her teeth.

She only asked me one question all night: Tell me again what your hubby does? I told her, again, that we weren't married, and explained his job, the organisation he worked for, the colleagues who formed our social circle. Just as I had done about Colette to the group at Oskar's, I found myself lightly dismissing these other people, sending up their habits, their harmless self-importance. Colette seemed interested – the only time, I realised, that she had really engaged with my conversation all evening – and asked whether they all did similar kinds of jobs, how long they had lived here, how much I thought they earned. How much does your husband earn? she asked.

I corrected her again, and she interrupted me to ask his name. I gave it, and then she asked his surname. I gave it again, feeling the same squirm of unease I'd felt when she finally left me at the door to my apartment. I wanted, suddenly, to undermine that feeling, and found myself confessing to her: I had struggled since we came here, to get to know people, to get below the surface of things. Colette seemed to expect such disclosures as her due; perhaps that's why mine had sprung forth so easily. She looked at me directly, that same small smile budding on her face. I find it hard to connect, I told her, my cheeks flaring, with this, well, with this community we're in. I hesitated over the 'we'. Do you ever find that? I asked her. I could hear how tedious my question sounded, what a well-worn track it scraped along. I wished I had said nothing.

Well, said Colette, I guess I've always found that I'm pretty popular.

Abruptly, she drained her drink and stood up to go. Don't want to get shitfaced, she said, meetings tomorrow morning. I'll walk you back.

We didn't speak much as we walked, Colette constantly tucking her hair behind her ears and sighing. God, this fucking wind, she said. Compared to how talkative she'd been when we first met, and during our uneasy trip to the flea market, this in-person silence felt taciturn. I was unnerved, having told myself I would no longer be unnerved by her.

So I'll come and meet you guys at Oskar's some time, she said as we parted at the bridge, and I can meet all the folks you've been telling me about. I told her, Yes, for sure, certain that I wouldn't. I said I would give her a shout when it was next happening.

*

I'm in a spiteful mood. Robin brought me home two sweet, inoffensive bunches of flowers. I thanked him limply, my eyes flickering pointedly to the white roses I had already trimmed and arranged in the blue jug on the mantelpiece. I listed the domestic tasks I've undertaken in a hectoring tone. I'm proud of this tone, but sorry, personally, because I know he is not the man, or not the type of man to whom this tone is really directed. In my head, I sourly set him some required reading before entering into any number of serious conversations about work, about the division of labour, about fear.

We have to choose, soon, about Robin's contract: whether it will be another year, and then possibly another year after that. His colleagues have assumed he'll take it, have assumed we want to stay; they all have. Best place to start a family, people have variously said to me. I have a general unease when I think about children, although their potential characteristics suggest themselves enthusiastically, in ways which are also a compliment to myself. It's difficult to pick out the practical edges of it all, of how another person would fit into this airless life, its preoccupations and minor obsessions, to imagine being the sustaining thing in someone else's life. I nickname the phantom children, casually – ghostly nuggets, pumpkins, pickles, lolling just out of sight, struggling to support their soft and fragrant heads. I know some of the women I went to school with have babies now.

When these kinds of conversations come up, I'm armed with facts and statistics. The percentage of income that goes on childcare, the dependency on a good support network. The impact on women's careers, the hours of domestic labour, the rage that comes with seeing how they are still divided. The two weeks' leave offered to male employees, by most companies. The relentlessly unspooling slack, and who picks it up.

But, I get told, things aren't as bad as that here. Not with this company, anyway. So, I get told, it's another reason to stay put.

It doesn't help that we live in a child-rich neighbourhood: every day I see women, the occasional man, lingering on the canal bridges and outside cafés, prams wedged beside them like small torpedoes, the ineffable human cargo within. In Robin's social circle, now, there are invitations to baby showers, to gender reveal parties. We went to one of these in the early weeks here, and watched with uncertain smiles as the mother-to-be cut a thick wedge in a white layer cake, almost dropping the knife in her excitement as a delicate blue sponge was revealed. The cake was perfect: sweet and lemon-scented, sandwiched with blackberry curd.

I feel as if I'm eating your baby, your little boy, I said to her later, three glasses deep into the complimentary prosecco. When we were undressing that night, Robin said, That was a weird thing to tell her.

*

Last night, I went to a gathering of the city's cultural organisations and embassies; speed dating had been arranged so that various parties could find out more about one another. I went with Nella (this was part of my duties, she made it clear, as a volunteer with the theatre), who hadn't registered in time to get us a date appointment, and so we lingered at the fringes of the general melee. She wanted to speak to someone from the Argentinian embassy and the British embassy, to talk about a potential tour for one of her shows, but she didn't know who they were, or what they looked like (I attempted to google the staff pages of the embassy websites, but couldn't get beyond the privacy notice). The name badges we were all wearing were poorly printed; even with rigorous peering, it was hard to discern a person's name, or the place they represented.

We fell into desultory conversation with a very good-looking blonde woman, severely coiffured. She chastised me for not speaking her language, then remarked on the room, the difficulty of these situations, twitching the lapels of her wool suit and scouring the crowd. She talked angrily about how there was so little provision for music education these days, so little understanding of how talent must be developed. It must be very challenging, I said. She plainly had as little interest in us as we had in her, although Nella clasped her shoulder several times in a civil attempt to deny this, before we drifted apart, mutually relieved. Nella quickly ate several handfuls of peanuts in a hard, spicy shell before we finally caught sight of the Argentinian representative. We waited to speak to him in a small queue for several minutes. When we came face to face, he struck me as being very out of it, though whether through jet lag or drink or just an access of diplomacy, it was hard to tell. I made some dull remark about the wine, and he reacted with a courteous hoot and a scrape backwards, as though making way for a towering wit. Nella asked him several commonplace questions which, he abruptly told us, we could have settled by email, and we left downcast, speaking briefly to a former cultural attaché of the Spanish embassy on our way out, who seemed similarly cloudy-eyed and prone to hyperbole. Perhaps it's embassy custom.

As we walked to the tram, Nella and I talked about a play we'd both seen recently, about domestic violence – it was two monologues, coming together in the final minutes. Afterwards there was a panel discussion. The male actor had affected a tweed flat cap in the intermission; his face was spliced with the shadow of its brim. His answers to the questions, to the chair's polite probing, were glib, but the students in the audience loved him, giggled at his weak jokes, remembered his name while the rest of the all-female panel were addressed as 'you'. Outside in the foyer, the artwork of a women's collective was displayed: graffiti-style prints splattered across with blood spray, children suspended in water.

*

To my own surprise, I met Colette again this week for a coffee, in the same café I'd seen her with Patrizia. She told me she'd looked Robin up, online. I'd told her his surname, and where he worked, so of course he'd be easy to find. She waited, smiling, for my reaction. Uneasy, I was unsure how to respond. I eventually said something feeble about how awful it was when you had to get employee photos taken, and she told me that a woman she used to work with had had a stalker who'd found her picture on her old workplace's website, then traced her on LinkedIn.

He used to wait across the road from her, she told me. He'd get a McDonald's or something, and just wait until she came out of the office, and then he'd walk behind her to her bus stop. He didn't get on with her, he just stood in the queue. The police couldn't do anything. They actually told her off for calling them. Waste of police time, that's what they implied. I said, What, even if he ends up murdering you? Well, she didn't like that. People never want to hear it.

I guessed this was all fanciful, but I half admired how elaborate the story was. I thought of my long-ago diary entries, the ravenous bears and wicked aunts. Clearly, I had nothing on Colette.

We all got used to seeing him out there, Colette continued, eating his burgers. In the end she stopped answering the office phone, she was so scared it might be him. Which was fucking annoying, Colette said, because we both worked on box office, and it meant I had to answer all the phones. I noted, surprised, the correlation of this small detail with one of her earlier stories. I was too timid to ask anything outright, to attempt to trap her, for once, into a hard fact. I came here with no ulterior motive, I had to remind myself.

I said that presumably, if the police weren't going to do anything, one of her colleagues would have walked with her to the bus stop every evening. To make sure she was OK. Presumably, said Colette. I've noticed that Colette talks about this kind of behaviour almost with amusement, as if it's something that exclusively happens to other people, to faintly foolish women. Her eagerness the night we first met, when she talked about the supposed men in the woods, is always resurfacing in her conversation: a friend or a relative of hers who's been followed, or touched, or had someone expose himself to them on public transport.

I responded to her story with my standard disgust, my sadness: everyone I know has had something like this happen to them. Or worse, Colette said. Or worse, I agreed.

Your hubby is so gorgeous, she said, changing tack. Like, really, really nice-looking. How long have you been together? Who asked who out?

I've stopped correcting her on the husband thing.

*

It's hard, I find it hard, as an adult, to abdicate responsibility for the things I did as a child. Other people, I know, have no problem with this; other adults have no problem in abdicating responsibility for the things they did as an adult, even in the quite recent past. But I think of certain moments, like the time I pinned my sister down and spat a long, chocolatey dribble into her open mouth; like the time I tipped my friend's little cow-shaped china jewellery dish off her dressing table on purpose, because she wouldn't let me play with her hair – and my heart contracts with shame. Why should I think like this? Why can't I move on? I think of the china fragments, the dampness of her little-girl fear, and I want to cry and snarl.

When I was very young, I had a friend called Mila. She was the new girl in my primary school class, and I was chosen to be her particular friend, to look after her and make sure she knew where everything was. I think the teacher chose me for this because she sensed our similarity – both slight, mousey children, with an unwilling manner. The toes of our patent button-over school shoes were scuffed from turning them inwards so often, trying to obviate attention.

Mila came to my house, and I went to hers. We played on the swings, made cards with glitter and block paint, baked cheese biscuits in the shape of horses. We played a game where each of us owned an imaginary puppy, and we had to tell one another how we'd decorated its basket, the leads and treats and accessories we'd bought for it. We sat together, taking it in turns to deliver these decorative monologues: her pretend puppy was called Toffee, and all of its things were coloured purple and silver. I wanted purple for my dog, and we argued over it; she called me a bitch, stuttering a little on the word.

We spent all our time together, referred to one another as 'best friends', were known to be inseparable by our teachers and parents, yet the whole time we shared an intense contempt for one another's company. This only found its outlet in rare instances – her calling me a bitch was the first. Another time, after midnight, in Mila's bedroom, during one of the sleepovers which our parents allowed us, we spent minutes in silent fury, tugging at each other's hair, hissing hot childish breath into each other's faces. Earlier in the evening, I had spilt my hot chocolate, deliberately, on Mila's sleeve, and quietly enjoyed the double misery of her pain and her dismay at her spoilt pyjamas, her favourite pair. When Mila's mother was sharp about her apparent clumsiness, Mila only shrugged, watching me silently while her mother rinsed the pyjama top in the sink. Another day, Mila shoved me, heavily, from a gatepost

I'd been standing on as part of a game, and I cracked my head hard against the pavement, rising to swab at a broad graze from which dark blood welled. When my parents asked me how I'd done it, I was mute. We knew where we stood, with this friendship. I judge most others by it.

Eventually, Mila's family ended up moving south, and I didn't see her again. I remember her mother made a big thing of us exchanging addresses, saying that we should write to each other, become pen pals, and that in the summer, I could come and stay with them for a few days, in their new house in Crawley. And I remember receiving Mila's first letter, printed on lilac paper. She had written I MISS YOU! In curly glitter script across the top of the page, and again on the borders. The rest of the letter I think was about horses. I never wrote back. When I asked my mother, years later, if she remembered Mila, she had to pause for a few moments before she could locate her – that small, nondescript child. She only lived in the town for something like four months, my mother told me, but the two of you, yes, you were great pals.

Four months. I wondered if I had imagined the intensity of that relationship; why was it I could still remember the exact texture of our dislike, the cool power of its mutuality? I could look Mila up, now – I remember her last name and it would be easy to find her, to unearth a little of what her life has been. But I can't do it. I want to keep her in that uneasy bubble of unknowing, the memory of her hair held taut in my fist.

*

Colette and I have now fallen into seeing each other about once a week, sometimes more. I am careful to always let her initiate these meetings, and I sense that she is very aware of this, and that it amuses her. At one point three weeks went by with nothing from her, until eventually I messaged her, asking whether she was in town. She didn't respond for two days, though I could see she had read the message, then sent me a picture of three ducklings in the canal.

We went back to the hot wings bar and I mentioned that I saw Patrizia the other day, not adding that I had seen her with Colette, a few weeks ago. I asked her whether she ever met up with any of the women from choir, socially. She didn't mention Patrizia at all, but talked enthusiastically about Monika – the woman who had originally warned me off Colette, months ago – about how they went on bike rides to the beach together, most weekends, and that she had been invited to Sunday lunch with Monika's family. Even in the teeth of the lie, I felt a dart of jealousy. I asked whether Monika had children and Colette told me she had two. She paused a moment, then told me they were a boy and a girl. Twins.

I told her that I remembered meeting Monika, the first and only time I went to choir, along with Patrizia. I asked whether Colette saw anything of her. Colette laughed in a way that conveyed she had been asked to keep a secret, and, not answering my question, told me that Monika and Patrizia did not get on. I asked how she knew, and she grinned at me and said, Gossip, gossip, in a scolding kind of tone. I realised this was a brush-off, and blushed, despite myself. This won't be true, I reminded myself: the Sunday lunches, the beach, none of it. Perhaps Colette knew that I was probing, that I was trying to catch her out. Though I wasn't, I told myself, I wasn't really.

I've become entranced by watching Colette in action: her self-assurance, her offensiveness, her perverse magnetism. There is a kind of anti-glamour about her, I thought, something that part of me recoils from while simultaneously wanting to get closer to. I remembered Mila, how briefly intense that relationship had been, how part of its closeness was founded on the knowledge of its fictiveness.

I talk more easily to Colette than I do to almost anyone else, apart from Robin. And yet it's not entirely natural, not the pull and tug of normal conversation. Sometimes when we meet, she asks me no questions at all, but rumbles on with anecdote after anecdote, herself at the centre of all of them: heroic and hard done by, by turns. Other times she peppers me with question after question: I've told her about my past jobs, about where I'm from, about my family. I've told her about my sister, about how she's something of a career girl back in London, a bit ferocious, and she told me instantly about her brother. I've heard about a brother a few times now: he never maintains the same personality across more than a couple of stories, but I've grown to be interested in him, even to ask solicitously after him, when Colette mentions him in passing. She hated him, she told me, he'd got round her stepdad, when he was dying, and got him to leave an apartment – a brownstone, she told me importantly – in New York, entirely to him, nothing for her. Her stepdad had been a famous artist, she told me, working in acrylic. He had lived in New York to be close to other artists, and to the best galleries.

Though he met your mum in New Zealand, presumably? I couldn't resist asking her. She met my eyes, unblinking. Actually, she said, Mum met Gary in the Middle East.

Colette told me there was only one thing you could do with siblings like ours – Cut them off, she said, don't respond, don't get involved. Let them know they can't take up space in your life. I was becoming used to hearing this scorched-earth policy from Colette, for people she didn't like, people she had difficulties with. When I thought of the vastness of continents supposedly separating her from her family, such a strategy didn't seem so wild. When I thought of the narrow strip of channel separating me from my sister, the proposed pulling down of the shutters seemed a lot more farcical. And besides, I told Colette, anxious that I'd got carried away, I don't want to stop talking to her, I like her, we just see things differently. We just wind each other up.

Colette, as so often, knew better than I did. It gets worse as you get older, she told me. You need to nip some people in the bud.

When I got home, Robin asked me how Colette had been. He refers to her humorously, now; he's caught my note of careful disdain. He doesn't understand why I still see her, when she's so obviously (I tell him) dislikeable, when she lies so consistently, so colourfully. I've only told him about the obvious lies, the many jobs she's supposed to have had, the bizarre things that have happened to her and her family and colleagues. He has the impression, now, that she's a character.

*

I've looked up the provincial towns and cities of note, so easy to reach, just a few hours by train – we'll knock these out one by one, I should think, over the summer. I also aim to be on nodding terms with those poorly maintained plaster models of Jesus, which loll in the countryside's ubiquitous small churches, with their spires like witches' hats. I think of the church I attended, sporadically, as a child: a half-embarrassed centre for the ceremonial. The steely autumn church suppers, the handfuls of us plumping down onto hassocks in confirmation class, raising literal clouds of dust.

My sister and I attended confirmation classes, largely because at the time my sister's best friend – a sudden, passionate relationship – was attending them, and my sister couldn't bear to be left out. Our parents had no strong feelings; it was a way to have us both out of the house on Sunday afternoons and they were satisfied that it was free, save a few pounds to be given for a special ceremonial candle, painted with our names. Mine ended up with a bite out of it – I suspected my sister, but could never prove anything.

The classes, led by the vicar, a man in his late forties, were delivered in accordance with a guidebook that lived on the shelf of the parish centre, where our lessons took place. We did not deviate from the suggested content – if the book said 'Now give ten minutes for discussion of the parable's meaning', ten minutes was what we had. At Halloween, there was disapproval at our bringing an orange-iced gateau, flecked with plastic spiders; we were only allowed to eat it if we referred to it as 'autumn leaf cake'. The class leader barely remembered our names from one class to the next and didn't bother to check if we had competed the sententious homework that was assigned to us each week. These were extracted from our own confirmation handbooks, which were different for boys and girls. Mine followed the story of a girl called Sasha, and took the form of a series of diary entries addressed to God and written in half-rhyme. In it she disclosed concerns about her parents, her sister, classroom pressures and anxiety about a friend who she felt might be self-harming. I never found out what the boys' handbook contained. Each of Sasha's diary entries ended with an exhortation to herself to perform some helpful task – do the dishes without being asked, wipe down the lunch tables at school.

I read the entries diligently, with distaste, while my sister defaced the cover of her handbook in biro, giving Sasha unimaginative devil's horns, as well as a handlebar moustache.

It wasn't their fault, or not completely, that they were so at a loss as to how to communicate with us. The whole situation was so abstract and embarrassing, and conducted with such necessary solemnity, that it brooked no honest discussion. Our sessions would be spent in rote, desultory conversation, and occasional trips to the altar to name and identify the objects we saw there. Once we were asked to join together in making a prayer; we had to write appropriate sentiments on scraps of paper and throw them into a large beige mixing bowl, which our leader whipped round and round with a wooden spoon and an inscrutable expression.

Shauna found the classes only boring, nothing more; she complained loudly every week about giving up her time to attend, she implied that even the vicar didn't believe what he was telling us. The friendship that had originally drawn both of us into the classes in the first place had soured a few weeks in, and the force of my sister's animus was such that her former friend had actually stopped coming to the classes, had joined a different group at a church in the suburb over. My parents wouldn't allow us to give it up, having become too accustomed to peaceful Sunday afternoons, radio on, the chicken browning luxuriously in the oven.

When I think of that childish discomfort, I'm thankful for how comfortably atheist this city feels to me, so many churches and cathedrals decommissioned, blank-walled and blank-eyed. The ugly red church in the centre of town is, inside, an expanse of unrelieved white space, now used only for gin festivals and corporate entertaining. Once a month, they do guided tours to the top of the bell tower, so you can look out upon the resolute flatness that surrounds you. Colette had commented on this, I remembered, in her casual dismissal of the country at large: I mean, she said, give me a prospect, you know?

When I was a child, a teacher once set us to drawing God – she described God as 'Him' – using our imagination. I drew God faintly, in pencil, standing on cloud, swathed in a sheet and with a curly beard, a thin grin and glass of sherry in his hand. In my mind, God was a comfortable conglomeration of Zeus and Father Christmas, benevolent and hedonistic. In our confirmation classes, we never questioned the view of God as male. At that time, I pictured him as a kind of grey and yellow cloud, angry-eyed. Violent and aggressive, the God of the Old Testament – of course he was a man. I didn't get many consoling visions of God from those classes, still less of his son, who seemed to us to be a kind of savant, a neurotic who came to his only possible end. I would have been one of the women in the crowd who tugged her veil about her and turned as the blood began to clot. As we grew older, a particular friend and I had arch conversations about the Church – we castigated it warmly, we supposed that Christ had been a real historical figure, but agreed simply that he had been the most prominent of a crowd of prophets and lunatics, who a freak course of events had elevated unimaginably. Now I'm not sure if that frightening vision, of the unhinged raver in the desert, the greasy hair and the fanatical eye, isn't really the image I would rather have.

*

We went to Oskar's again last night. I didn't invite Colette, and spent the whole evening looking over my shoulder, anxious that she might appear. Robin told me to relax, and someone asked whether I was waiting for someone. She's keeping an eye out for her stalker, Robin said, and I batted his arm. This is someone who doesn't come to the stuff I invite her to, I said, that's the opposite of a stalker.

I know why I didn't ask Colette to come. Not because I'm worried she'll give away to the others what I'd said about them, my light bitchiness. Not because of her oddness, not because I'm worried that she'd instantly start on some peculiar story that would make all the others here look at each other and grin, though I pretend to Robin that this is the case. When I was tossing it up, whether to message Colette, to ask her, again, to join us, the image of her and Patrizia sitting together came to my mind. Patrizia smiling and nodding, Colette's friendly arm close to hers. She's busy anyway, I lied to Robin. She's out of town this weekend.

*

I've been on a culling spree of small objects since we moved here. Unpacking dinky bowls, novelty ornaments and small, cheap jewellery caskets, studded with coloured glass and diamantes. I've hefted most into the bin, feeling no pangs at the resurgent memories of who had given what, and on what occasion. Though I used to love clutter – the surfaces of my room at home were so thick with carefully positioned junk that it was impossible to clean anything, and so my various porcelain mice, moneyboxes, salt dough figurines, all stood gravely in their own little pools of dust. Solid objects, an amassing against a coming tide of destruction. Now there are only one or two trinkets here, although sensitively placed: a miniature jug, spotted with green roses, kept more for the memory of its disproportionate expense than for any liking.

A sea-blue bowl shaped like a fish. I have to be careful, though, have to guard against the slow creep of stuff. The other day, for instance, Robin bought me a sheep-shaped keyring, which bleats when you press its tail, and stares with yellow lit-up eyes. It sits eyeing me at my desk for now, but it will have to make its forced exile at some point. It's this kind of pathetic ruthlessness that leaves my mind very clear, very satisfied. You begin to see the attraction of tyrannies on a larger scale.

*

Sometimes I feel like I live in some cosmic gumball machine, whipped sickeningly through the stale air in a route practised, but still terrifying. Waiting for the coin to make its final rattle, the bright planets to drop.

This also isn't true. When I was younger, all I wanted was to stay in one place for the rest of my life. I thought the ultimate vision of happiness would be to wake up, every morning, in a bed that overlooked the familiar green spaces, that I would walk to my work, whatever it was, through the silver-grey town, eat my lunches in the same park where I had dangled from the iron fretwork of the railings as a child, go every autumn to the same firework display, go every December to watch the Christmas tree lights blink on in the square. And my children, wherever they sprang from, would fit into the quiet pattern of that life.

I imagine myself, now, on a March or April afternoon, buying ingredients for the evening meal. I imagine walking past my child's school to reach the supermarket and feeling deep, lemon-scented peace at knowing him there, cradled in the belly of raised arms, green jumpers and lunchboxes. I think of Robin and I making plans to attend the small market outside the church on Saturday morning, our daughter springing between us. Imagine not cringing inside my own skull on a Sunday evening, my hair hopelessly clean, my pyjamas stiffening on the radiator. I didn't always want to be safe from that.

That phrase: a quiet life. I have grown up in one kind of pastoral while being stuffed with images of another: the result is an enduring hunger for the kind of life their collision would represent. I was raised – strange phrase that is, as if I was a new loaf, springing into wholesome fullness – in a small town, a dim stone set in the muscular green and blue of almost-wild coast and countryside. The ancient past bristled in ubiquitous leaflets and shop names, but was much harder to sense in the texture of everyday life, although as an adult, I have pretended otherwise, I've gestured, furtively, to some streak of that dark and mystic green-ness, never authentically felt.

What I mean is, you can grow up and go to school and watch Nickelodeon and eat jelly worms and go to the swimming pool and buy small colourful badges to skewer your jackets and use the vending machine in the post office on Saturdays, all the time feeling that mysterious, chthonic tug. But the busy, colourful plastic presence of the first dissipates the power of the second, it embarrasses it. And you become so fond of the first, because that in turn becomes the original collage of nostalgia – when I go back home, back to the coast, I want to walk past the old swimming pool, now turned into flats, I want to stand in the kitchen of my friend's house, and be served orange juice in the same piglet-patterned glass. The idea of this is a fierce pleasure, a longed-for, sustaining breath. It would be unbearable, not to have that promise of return, of replenishment.

Perhaps I don't feel any of this. All my life, there has been this small layer of embellishment, a fringe to soften the edges of the hyper-real. Sometimes the lies are so small they exist only as a fine haze – more a series of small imprecisions than lies. And some things, as the cliché goes, I have told and re-told so often, with small alterations, fine daubings and re-touchings, that I genuinely cannot give the original version, even to myself. It becomes harder to sift out the grains of truth – or reality – from the mud of fiction.

If I'm after one bead to build myself around, Colette has fashioned herself a whole string of them. The last time we met she was still mentioning her time in Auckland, although her mother has now faded from the picture. She also spoke this week, at length, about London, once she found out I'd lived there. Again, it was hard to separate what might have been an out-and-out lie from grains of truth: she named various Tube stops, not the obvious ones, without hesitation; she mentioned a tiny Thai restaurant in Camberwell which did indeed exist: I'd once been to it with Shauna and her boyfriend, who'd talked doggedly about bitcoin while my sister tried to take surreptitious photographs of a minor celebrity sitting in the corner. I told Colette that I knew it and must have sounded surprised because she laughed, curtly. Well yeah, she said, I do get around.

*

Today, after a week of silence, Colette started sending me pictures of cats. Or rather the same cat, in different positions. She didn't send any commentary, or explanation, just cat after cat after cat.

After an hour or so, feeling foolish, I messaged her: Did you get a new cat? She responded with another picture, and told me it was her neighbour's; she was looking after it while they're on holiday.

I replied, lamely, Sweet. The next picture she sent me was a selfie, her holding and gripping one of the cat's paws in a pretended high-five. A small bubble of envy rose and popped in my brain. I asked her if she wanted to meet up. She was cool in her replies: Sure, she said. Not this weekend, but one evening next week? Thursday.

I agreed, and then felt stumped. I did not, definitely did not, want to invite her here, the apartment that I find small and comforting and lonely and insufficient and above all *ours*; I did not want her here, looking at my collection of mugs and the row of postcards tacked up on the back of the door, and the fading stripes of our cushions, bought years ago from a market stall in Chester, and much spilt-on. I didn't want Colette's cool, bright, false gaze falling on any of this.

I dithered, phone in hand, until Colette's next message buzzed through with a suggestion to meet at her apartment. I instantly accepted, and then felt bad-tempered for the rest of the evening.

*

Colette's apartment was not what I'd expected. I'd imagined some clean and characterless shell, perhaps tastelessly decorated, with cream walls and a kitchen-cum-dining room: the pattern followed by most of the apartments I'd been in so far, the apartments of Robin's colleagues, the friends of their friends. Colette's was closer in style to my own: older, creakier, doors and frames painted a sticky spinach colour, inside an abundance of wooden stairs and panelling, all loopy with knots and ill-fitting planks.

She was one of those hosts who affected to forget that she was, in fact, a host. She received me with ill grace, as though I'd interrupted her in something, although I couldn't see what this might have been. The TV was off, her laptop closed. There was nothing cooking in the kitchen. Yet she gave an impression of faint huffiness, agitation. I had to ask her if I could have something to drink, although this was more to break the awkwardness between us. I felt like saying, sulkily, you *asked* me here – before I remembered the faint tension of our last exchange, and my own prevarications. Looking around for something to compliment, I told her that I liked her kitchen table, small, wooden, with an intricately carved base which I knew, from experience, would be dreary to dust. But Colette was resistant to the compliment: Everything here, she told me immediately, belonged to the landlord; really. She couldn't call anything in the place her own. The books, I suggested, noticing a shelf of brightly-coloured paperbacks –

Left behind, she told me abruptly, by previous tenants. All of them were in Dutch, except a copy of *Harry Potter and the Prisoner of Azkaban*. And she didn't like Harry Potter.

I asked her if she liked reading, realising that none of our previous conversations had ever touched on books. I love it, she replied, fiercely, at once. I love it.

I asked her what she liked to read; I heard myself putting on my book-club voice. Colette mentioned an author I'd never heard of, and talked at length about the plot of her latest novel, set in France during the Resistance. I listened politely, and asked if I could borrow it when she'd finished it. She told me that wouldn't be possible, because she'd already promised to lend it to another friend.

She has been different with me, I thought, almost every time we've met. So unctuous at first, then slyly self-deprecating, then brusque and dictatorial. Her speech has coarsened as well. She's been trying out different guises on me, I considered. The thought was almost flattering. I wondered which version of Colette Patrizia was given, which one Monika was given, if any of that was true. I wanted to know how Colette, as a person I had spent time with, by now more time than anyone else I'd met here, truly thought of me. I wanted a response, and surprised myself with the intensity of this longing, the frustration that it looked for an answer in the one person who I knew would never give me a straight one.

I stayed another hour; enough time to drink two glasses of wine, unwillingly poured, and make more stilted conversation about books, about the neighbourhood. I had thought Colette would be gleeful at having me in her house, that her hospitality would be effusive. I thought the worst thing about the visit would be having to shield myself from her overbearing manner, from conversation that would become stickily confiding. But it was almost the opposite; I felt, as the visit went on, the faint embarrassment of being unwelcome, and unsure how to gracefully remove myself. I felt the sullenness of a relationship that is conjured, by each person, into something more interesting than it really is. I had enjoyed thinking there was something monstrous about Colette that I could interrogate, mopping up the tainted juices of her character that seeped helplessly from her, as I thought I had discerned at our first meeting. But this, this chilly, desultory chat, both of us flicking glances at our phones, had no savour or interest, even the interest of distaste. I thanked her for the hospitality, said it had been lovely to see her flat and left. We didn't say anything about when we might next meet.

Summer

Today I thought about shopping lists and outfits. I thought about my body and how I should feed it. I have been dutifully following the advice, to check myself in the shower, to get to know my body. I pass sudsy hands over my breast and wonder what it is I'm looking for – there seem to be strange islands of flesh in there, swellings and nodules that sometimes feel uniform, one breast to the other, one day to the next, and sometimes not. Sometimes an inflamed lump appears in my armpit – I put it down to a dirty razor. Who can point me to the correct procedure, here? Whose is the master body, against which I can tally my findings?

*

I bumped into Colette in town today. Almost literally; I was coming out of the library, my supermarket list ready, when she loomed suddenly in front of me in the revolving door. I backtracked, went and stood with her beside the tourist information desk. She took some time detaching a thin rainbow-coloured scarf from her neck – it had become tangled with her earring – and spoke to me surlily, as though I was the cause of this irritation. I asked if she was here to take a book out and she told me no, she needed to use the computers, needed to print something. Unless you have a printer, she asked, suddenly. I lied that I didn't (or not quite a lie – it isn't my printer, or at least I didn't buy it).

I asked Colette what she needed to print and she told me it was notes for a presentation, and handouts, for those that would be there. I asked what the presentation was about and she blustered, told me it was something very specialised in human resources. I remembered that I'd thought, when we first met, that she might work in HR, and was impressed at my prescience before I caught myself: this was Colette. I asked her where her offices were and she ignored me.

Let's see how long it takes, she said, let's see how long it fucking takes to get some printing done, here. All these computers take a thousand years to crank up. I demurred feebly; they were actually pretty good, and I said something vague about how I found public services, on the whole, to be very good in the Netherlands. Oh yeah, said Colette, oh yeah. She held her scarf between her hands, pulling it taut, and started to flip it like a skipping rope. I left her there, glowering at a set of leaflets for a water park. In the supermarket, I kept glancing around; I couldn't shake the sense that she was shadowing me, angrily, between the aisles.

*

I keep saying we should have another party, after the success, or at least after the non-failure, of our Christmas gathering. I say it mostly because I know, again, it's only Robin's colleagues we can reasonably expect to invite, and so the stakes, for me, are low. If the thing doesn't go well, he would have the embarrassment of an immediate meeting, whereas I can pick and choose when and if I'll see the guests again. That makes me enthusiastic.

Robin asked me the other evening what would make me happy. I thought of the aborted list in my notebook, of how I might shift about these prospective pockets of contentment, like stacks of gambling chips. I suggested we go to the cinema more.

His contract here will finish in another year, although in all likelihood this will be extended. He wants, I know, to go further afield: there are jobs available with the same company in Singapore, in Beijing. Some of the others in his office, the people we meet at Oskar's, and at weekends, in one another's apartments, have the same idea. I'm not saying, he told me, that we'd just transplant everything from here to there.

I told him he hadn't listened, but I can't tell him what it is he's meant to have missed. I said to him, I don't like the idea of going backwards, but I'm unsure, now, what backwards means. He thinks I mean going back. What you're doing now, you could do from anywhere, he said to me. We could live anywhere.

I told him I didn't know where I wanted to live. I said, in a silly voice, that I wanted to live in a little hole, like a mouse, with a leaf to cover me, and that ended the conversation.

*

In the library again today. At the first desk I sat at, the man behind me coughed and snorted with so much evident phlegm that I had to move after only an hour. The next desk was fine for another hour, but then two students descended a few places along from me and started receiving frequent, boisterous phone calls, which they were invariably obliged to answer, despite their censorious greeting to each caller: Fucking hell, man, you know I'm in the library!

I noticed several students in – or close to – tears; some being comforted by a friend, others sniffing silently, headphones in. I guessed it must be the pressures of exams; I thought of my own brief and frenzied bouts of study and composition. Some people boasted of spending all night in the library, dipping under their desks in the small hour for a few grim hours' respite beneath a duffel coat, or foul-smelling sleeping bag. Although few ever actually lived up to this show of incredible work ethic.

The one person I knew who did had almost exhausted himself in his efforts at school, and pretty much went to pieces when he got to university. It's clear now that it was some kind of obsession with Gareth – he would fill page after page of notebooks with colour-coded notes, scribbling in utterly exhaustive detail about every aspect of a given subject. If he was implored to truncate his display of learning, he would literally scream. He frightened me slightly; in other ways I found him fascinating and fearless. He cultivated a moody and enigmatic presence on Facebook, which intrigued me, because I was never able to countenance such a public persona myself. I couldn't bear the idea that people might see things about me, which I supposed they supposed would come straight from the heart, and judge me accordingly; it was a notion I found upsetting to contemplate, it was a piece of pure existential pain that I could not quietly confront. At that age, and even now, to some extent, the fear of other people's opinions trailed me like a small shrieking dog; I had to physically scrunch up my eyes and mutter yerrsh or hmmmm to dispel it. It was why I would answer a question in class and then rage silently to myself cunt, cunt, cunt.

I hear from Gareth only occasionally; he is bad at keeping in touch. I went to his flat once for dinner. At the time he was living with a boyfriend, Liam. Gareth was making a prawn curry and I had to tell him, mortified, that I was allergic to shellfish. That's fine, said Liam quickly, absolutely fine. The prawns will keep till tomorrow, he pleaded. Gareth smiled very tightly and said absolutely nothing, but dumped a tin of chickpeas into the pot. I knew what gales of rage and blame would ensue when I left, could imagine the words with which Liam would attempt to console.

When Gareth and I do meet now (always for a carefully prescribed length of time, always in public), he is fiercely brittle and studiedly uninterested in my own life, its small triumphs and passing interests. Liam has long fled. He adopts a homely, conservative attitude that might be mildly amusing if played for laughs, but with him I think that, once performed as a shield from the crueller aspects of the outside world, it has now calcified into belief. Gareth is not at home in the world; the world, he once told me, is a sickening place. He refers, quite unselfconsciously, to 'youths'; he sneers at their music and clothes, he derides their drinking. I once asked after another man he had been close to at university – I'd met this friend once or twice, and I had liked him well enough. But Gareth said that he had turned out to be a false friend, two-faced and conniving. It was sad, he told me with an air of prescience, how people could betray you like this.

*

For some time now I've been the one messaging Colette with no replies. I've sent her pictures of the things I see, on my daily walks. I've sent pictures of the cat who sits on the balcony opposite mine, remembering her earlier barrage of cat pictures, thinking this would elicit a response – it didn't.

She's dropped me I think, I said to Robin, covering my discomfort with a laugh. Good, he said, I'm glad. Now you can just hang around with the normal people. You do realise, he went on, I've never actually met her? But you've seen her, I said, you've seen her talking to me outside the flat. I believe she exists, he said, I meant that you've never introduced us.

I turned away from him, opening the cupboards to look for a packet of spaghetti. I thought you had no interest in meeting her, I said. *You* think she's weird.

You think she's weird, he said. She is weird, or she sounds weird. I only mean, you've met all the people I hang out with, and I haven't met her.

I said that Colette preferred to meet one-to-one. She doesn't sound shy, he said, and I told him it wasn't about shyness. Not everything has to happen in a group, I told him, where there's never any interesting conversation. I bit my lip at my own dissembling; I couldn't have an interesting conversation to save my life.

*

I went again to see the theatre group this morning. We hadn't been in touch for some time; I'd got the sense that they were beginning to realise my limitations, as a non-Dutch speaker, in helping them to promote their work, which, as English-heavy as all their press and social media is, still demands a better grasp of the local context to oil the wheels. I felt that this meeting would be some sort of kindly-meant brush off. The day was hot, and I could feel the sun pulling the blood into the back of my neck, my bare shoulders, as I walked the twenty minutes from my apartment to the theatre to meet them. The smell of sulphur thickened the air whenever I passed a canal; it hung greenly beneath the stone bridges.

When I arrived, I found that their temporary building had been, unexpectedly, stripped in the night – not robbed, but some official-seeming hired hands had come and dismantled the kitchen fittings and removed all the tables and chairs (save those in their office). They were polite about it, Nella told us, but they made it clear that the order for a full de-commissioning of the building could come at any day, tomorrow maybe – or else it might not come for two years. I said I would find that very difficult, the uncertainty, and the worry of wondering where to go next, and how to afford it (they rent their office space at a fantastically reduced rate). But Nella didn't seem too bothered – she fussed as usual around the hot plate, making coffee and whisking warm milk, and searching determinedly in the cupboards to unearth a bag of biscuits to accompany our meeting. The emptied, echoing building filled me with disquiet, and I had a vision of some rogue figure bursting in with a weapon, after the building's copper piping. That would be a strange way to die, not quite in the name of art. Nella was scornful about this country and its insular ways; she bemoaned a lack of generosity in its approach to international culture, in its willingness to share ideas and contacts and time. That is the arts, all over, I blagged, and she nodded grimly: I know it.

In the end, they didn't ask me outright to stop working – to stop volunteering – for them. Nella spoke vaguely about it being a quiet period, about things being uncertain, because of the premises situation. I expressed my concern, my understanding, formulaically. When I got up to leave, Nella tied up the bag of biscuits and placed it in my hands. Something to take with you, she said.

*

Robin and I were putting away the shopping, him telling me about his day, the dog that someone had brought into the office, the resulting ill-feeling over someone else's allergies. Also, he said, I think I bumped into her today. Her, your friend. Or your not-friend, rather. Colette. My stomach swooped. Where? I said, trying to appear casual. I stacked two tins of tomatoes on top of one another, slid them sideways in the cupboard to make way for a third. What did she say? Did she mention me?

Just opposite the café at the end of Witstraat, Robin said. She was waiting for someone. She didn't say anything, particularly; I mean, she said she recognised me, she said she'd seen me with you before.

She's seen your picture, I thought, on the company website. How did she seem? I asked. Robin shrugged. Normal, he said, I mean she didn't say much. It wasn't, you know, it wasn't an interesting encounter. He nudged me lightly. She didn't follow me or anything! But now I know that she's real. I mean, I know you're not making her up.

Ha, I said sourly, obviously not. But she really didn't say anything else? I shunted a litre of vegetable oil into the corner and shut the cupboard door. She didn't ask you anything?

No, said Robin, she just said she was meeting a friend. What was she supposed to ask me? I'm just her mate's boyfriend. Not mate, sorry. She didn't seem like much of a stalker.

She's not a stalker, I said patiently, I never said that.

What is she playing at? I think. And then I catch the taint of paranoia in the thought. What did I expect: for her to trail Robin home, for her to be waiting in the apartment for me when I returned? Smug and ensconced, with Robin rapt at her decisive conversation; or appalled by her synthetic chumminess. I can't tell if the image is unwelcome, and then tell myself to stop this. What am *I* playing at?

*

At the weekend, Robin and I went to a house-warming for a new employee, somebody who'd just transferred from Brussels. It was held at a ground-floor apartment, in an unknown quarter of the city. Through the hall, one enormous room complete with heavy wooden table, perfectly appointed chrome and ceramic kitchen, and then through the French windows to a yard fizzy with fairy lights and greenery.

We ate rapidly cooling nachos, grafted together by thick scabs of cheddar. The woman I initially sat next to, Lana, talked pruriently about the dangers of the wood at night, reminding me of Colette. This same woman went on to say that her teenage son was in Berlin at the moment with a friend – 'a model' – and had been invited to a party at a nightclub, VIP access, all for free. His mother was suspicious. You don't get anything for free, do you, Lana gloomed. I pointed out that, in inviting a model, the nightclub gained attractive, envy-inducing clientele who would, in turn, attract more paying punters. It's just marketing. Lana twitched. You don't get anything for free, she insisted. I gave up on her and turned to my host, who was by this point pleasantly drunk and confiding. His partner, Jakob, had adopted towards him a world-weary, forbearing attitude, tainted with amused contempt. More fizz? Jakob smiled, topping us both up. We talked about settling in. Several people asked me if I have found anything to *do* yet, and I said lightly that it's frustrating when people assume I'm lolling aimlessly at home. Jakob immediately corrected me. People mean to be kind by it, he pronounced; they're interested, and trying to be helpful. I said, Of course, of course, and picked at another tortilla chip, by now cold and slimed with a film of guacamole.

Jakob wasn't drinking; he said he if drank he would only talk pessimistically about his ex-boyfriend, which he did anyway. I told him it didn't bother me: negative conversation into which I can interject indignantly and sympathetically is my forte; really my only conversational mode. I then talked for a while to his current partner, Karl, who interrupted a joke about beachwear to tell me that I was such *a kind listener*; he repeated it and pressed my hand as he did so, at which I could only smile and say, Yes yes, very gently, regretting that I hadn't thought to time a toilet break in line with this tonal shift. Later in the evening another woman asked, very deferentially, if she could touch my tasselled earrings. I quite understood; I have a small mania for weighing masses of fine silver chains and the like, myself.

Lana asked me whether I'd made any Dutch friends, and I said that I hadn't yet. Before I could think about it, I'd mentioned Colette. I met her at a choir, I said, do you know her? She didn't, nor did she know Patrizia, or Monika. It's nice that you met someone through a hobby, Lana told me, I feel I only ever meet people through work, now. I didn't tell her that I'd only been to the choir once; that my relationship with Colette had a bloomed on it like mould, that I didn't believe the things she told me, but no longer found this problematic; that I was envious of Colette, the stories she made of herself, around herself, the confidence it gave her.

Temper

We should all try harder, Lana told me, to get to know other people.

*

I was cycling home this afternoon when I saw Colette standing at the tram stop. She was talking to a woman and when I turned at the crossing, I saw that it was Monika. I almost stopped, but kept pedalling; I glanced back and saw they were talking. I couldn't be sure, but it looked as if Colette had her hand on Monika's arm. I couldn't make out Monika's expression.

Well, I said to Robin later, this was the same woman who warned me off her. Said she'd been harassing her.

Maybe they just ended up at the same tram stop, he said. You don't know what they were actually saying.

It didn't look like that, I told him. It didn't look like that at all. I felt weirdly angry, hurt. And if I said anything to Colette, what would she say? Just that yes, of course, she was talking to Monika, a friend, a friend who she goes to the beach with, who invites her for Sunday dinner. I could show her the messages Monika sent me, all those months ago. But I won't, I know with a sudden tiredness, do any such thing.

*

Day and night, swarms of trivia occupy me, the bottom of the casserole dish looms large again, coins of carrots roll endlessly – and yet I am suspicious of this self-generated preoccupation, as something keeping me from real business, whatever that is. Robin has asked me again to think about *next steps*: that's what it is.

Inventing nonsense to exhaust my mind, keep me away from good work, from proper thought. Acts of self-sabotage. In London I didn't have to sabotage myself. Work, the sourness and pettiness of the office, the discomfort, the restraint, the commute, the dirty air – the attrition of all this, which is no more than the absolute normal, and far better than most – was enough to daily stunt my good intentions, my larger ambitions around writing. I would struggle to retain them, piecemeal: a slow-birthed story on a blank Sunday afternoon, the fortnightly writing class where interest was briefly rekindled, all plots dutifully applauded. And the welcome Friday and Saturday nights spent discussing the supposed work, the supposed direction, with other people, with people our age. We pepped each other up; we were experts in pep. None of it was falsely meant; it was just the time – we weren't going to quite get around to it yet, obviously not – the office, the Tube, the brief weekends away, the gym – obviously not. And now here, I take a deep breath every morning as I sit down at my desk: here comes the mind, whistling to its own merciless timetables, its aisles unswept, its seats grimy with the sweat of a thousand pointless concerns.

*

I saw Colette in town this morning, looking into the window of a clothes shop. My eagerness overtook me, I called her name and indicated that I would come over. I immediately went to cross the road, checking, in an exaggerated way, for traffic.

She smiled tightly at me. Hey, she said. What's up? I asked her if she was clothes shopping. I'm actually waiting for my friend, she said, she's in there at the moment. Her cousin's twenty-first birthday is coming up, and she wanted to get something new. It's sad, actually, she went on, it's so sad, because the cousin has sickle cell anaemia, and they don't know whether this is the last birthday, or what. So they want to go all out.

I peered past her into the shop, which had no customers in it, and was too small to have a changing room. It's bigger upstairs, Colette said. Are you heading somewhere?

I was only heading home, and didn't like to say so. It was great to see your apartment the other day, I said. Actually, I've been meaning to return the favour. Do you want to come round some time? I asked. Are you free on Thursday evening, maybe?

Colette blew her cheeks out. My friend's here for a few days, she said. So maybe after that? I'll send you a message.

I said to her, suddenly, that we might be leaving soon, that Robin might not extend his contract. We hadn't actually discussed this, properly; I hadn't said such a thing to anyone else.

No way, Colette said, are you? She said it in the same tone Jo had used, months ago, when I first told her about Colette: a pretence of interest, a backnote of dismissal.

She made a movement towards the door of the shop. I'm going to check on her, make sure she's not got a zip stuck or anything, she said. I'll see you later.

I looked at Colette, the smug contours of her face, daring me to contradict her. The ruse was such a feeble one, clearly not beneath her dignity, only beneath mine.

Wrong-footed, I stood locked on my square of pavement. I have never touched her, I realised, not ever: never placed a confiding hand on her shoulder, or brushed my cheek against hers in greeting. You're not telling me the truth, I said to her. I can see nobody's in there. Why are you telling me there is?

My frustration built, a green tide rising through my body, a menthol flush that stained my cells, scrubbed my vision, singed my mind. I thought of all the blunted alleys my every foray, every attempt to connect, had turned into; they throbbed in my mind like a deck of stubbed toes. I thought of Mila and Shauna, of kind, pitying Jo, of this inchoate restlessness in which I was suspended, out of which they had found an exit.

It erupted over my lips, this confused spew of hurt: Stop it!

Colette jumped backwards. For the first time, I saw a naked expression of surprise in her eyes: no guile, no condescension, no private curtain of calculation.

Why do you do this? Why do you make up all this stuff? I wasn't used to confrontation and struggled at first to find its register. My heart heaved, the skin on my face fat and numb with hostility. I moved towards her, unthinking. I grabbed her wrist.

I need you to lower your voice, Colette said with quiet authority, I need you to let go of me, right now. It sounded like the kind of thing that you learnt on a course – how to diffuse a situation with someone unhinged. Colette was calm, quasi-official: she's been here before, I realised. I stared at her; I understood that I wasn't the first person to call her out. Not even that, I thought.

Colette watched me. Maybe this is a good thing, she said. We probably shouldn't see each other for a while. I caught her eye, tried to hold it but she tossed her head, made a show of looking behind her, into the shop. Fine, I said, fine. I was still holding her wrist, could feel the tiny, unbothered tick of her pulse.

Colette shook her head at me, as if in sadness, and that small smile, the smile that said she knew everything, and dismissed it, reappeared, the momentary surprise caught and suppressed. And why not, I thought, for a hopeless second, why not inhabit a lie, wear it proudly, a second skin. Then: You're a liar, Colette, I said to her. The word had been poised like a dart on my tongue for its final flight, drawing some poison with it. And the heat that had been building in my skin crept into my eyes: I felt my vision blurring. You're a liar, I said again. She gently detached my fingers from her wrist.

Take care now, Colette said to me, as if I were someone much older, or a person who'd been unwell. She crossed the threshold of the shop.

The adrenaline I'd felt began to ebb out of me; its chemical backwash made me feel frail. I pretended to check my phone, I clucked my tongue in mock annoyance, hoping to deflect any lingering stares from people on the street who might have heard us, might have seen me grab Colette's wrist.

On the way back to our flat, mind a protective blank, I rounded a corner and saw Monika, standing outside a bar. I was about to hurry past her – we'd only met once, in person, only had that brief text exchange – but she stopped me, smiled, asked how I was doing. I stood with her for a moment. Unguarded, I told her what

I'd been moved to tell Colette: that we were thinking of moving, of making a change.

Good for you guys, she said easily. We're thinking of doing the same, you know. I've been feeling, there's something – she flapped her hands around, taking in the bar behind her, the milling street, the city itself – just something, I don't know. She couldn't articulate it, but I recognised, at once, the small pulse of discontent. She smiled at me again, took her sunglasses off and tucked them neatly into the neckline of her shirt. She looked me full in the face, her expression clear. Good luck to you, she said.

At home, I gave Robin an edited version of my encounter – I described it as the final one – with Colette.

Did she bother you that much? Robin asked me. Did she really? I think you should be glad she's dropped you. I mean, everything you tell me about this woman is off, it's weird. Even her name is weird.

Colette, I said, it's French. And don't just say, well, she's not French.

She's not, though, said Robin. And it doesn't sound like a real name to me.

I didn't say that I'd told Colette, told Monika, that we were thinking of leaving, of moving on, moving out – being elsewhere. But now that I've said it out loud, now that I've said it to them, I feel clearer about it, suddenly. Something about them both – Colette's dismissal, Monika's quiet valediction – has shifted something in my mind. Not more of the same, I think, and not back.

I had thought at one time like the woman in that training workshop, with her matching accessories and prophetic stare, that life would always be forward motion. Nothing in reverse. But now I feel as if I've already lapped myself on this circuit; sometimes at night, not sleeping, I feel my elbows sawing, breath coming thick and pointless as the same thoughts reappear. And Colette standing there, dinging the bell of her indifference, has brought this home.

When Mila told me she was moving away, I can't remember what my reaction was. I wonder, in fact, if she actually ever told me she was; whether it wasn't left to my mother to share the news, pacify me, to ease the supposed shock of parting. The joy of parting. I know I never answered her letter, the one with the glitter and the horses. Something obscene about it, I think now, a written testament to a brand of friendship that wasn't the one we had, that had never existed.

*

What thousands and millions of pounds, what great chunks of others' professional and personal time, what concessions and unhappinesses in perfect strangers, all this life will take up and absorb. In my most detached moments, I can't see that there is anything to make such a fuss over. I will live and live, and die and die. I don't need to feel more rarefied, more anxious, more absorbed in sustaining the soft inner yolk of my imperilled wellbeing, by being fed that modish fiction. That's not, as they say, my truth. And it seems to be born from a defensive, really a negative position. It has to assume the presence of constant and indiscriminate forces of hate for its sustenance; without these, the whole movement would be bewildered, would shrivel to a sorry horn-parp, a discarded, besloganed T-shirt. And I believe in the forces of hate, don't get me wrong, of course I do. But it's the approach that renders them indiscriminate that I have a problem with – if the malevolent force is homogenised, then isn't it also fatally underestimated? I don't talk this way in real life, you understand.

*

It's increasingly hard to work out whether this – whatever this is, a diary, a journal, some kind of record-keeping, a statement for the record – is the sort of thing a person, a proper person, would or should be doing, partly because I find my real-world self detaching, ever so gently, from the mother ship of my essential character. Not floating away, exactly, but certainly drifting some way ahead, or behind, tethered by a thin red rope. Not that the rope is fraying, not completely. But it is slackening. The solitude again, exacerbates this process, with few people to measure myself against, to bring that hard silver chink of contact and comparison that instructs a purpose, or at least an action which may be usefully disguised as purpose.

Yesterday, to fill a blank chunk of evening, I went upstairs and hung out of the window to smoke. It had been hailing, unseasonably, and the roofs and the red brick street looked clean and sharp. The top-floor windows around me were lighted, but no one else was looking out, certainly no one else had the idea to stand and hawk smoke over the window ledge. As I stood there a taxi drew up directly below me and a couple got out, arguing faintly. I got the impression they were returning from their holidays, and felt their bad-tempered fatigue, like a scented steam, rising to reach me where I lolled above, peering intently. It's much easier to make this kind of return alone.

I think about Colette, I think about what I'm doing here, I think about how to make things work, in a way that's different to the way that Robin's colleagues, that Jo, that Li, that Gareth, and even Colette, make things work, make things bearable. It takes up energy, it takes up time; the time I originally thought I had so much of. I stammered twice on the phone yesterday; I replied to an email a full day later than I was capable of doing. This dereliction is both something I can't afford to do, literally can't afford, and something I know also to be very bad for my psyche, my personal development, my still mulchily forming character, my current and future networks, my reputation, my self-justification, my family, my pub conversation, my Christmas dinner conversation, my body and my soul. I thought being here would tether me to something, would weight me, in the absence of other ballast. I haven't formed a single honest relationship; there is no one of any real meaning in my orbit who wasn't already there the day we arrived, spilling our small and untidy lives onto the unevenly varnished boards, wincing at the swooping angles of the bedroom ceiling.

Colette was someone who might have counted, a small and inscrutable planet who might still have expanded a smaller universe. I think now how my original smug dismissal of her seemed to leach from me to her, to be reflected back. I don't feel ghosted so much as haunted, not by Colette, not by her rich and meaty self, but by the figment of friendship; the grey pressure of a connection lost, an agent that might have thickened a texture of this life. After all, I had learnt nothing, gained nothing from her: she remained a cipher I had no interest, any more, in breaking.

*

Robin has told me we need to make the choice, now, about whether we stay. If I keep putting off the discussion, he said, it'll get decided for us. He meant, it would get decided for him, and me by extension. I'd forgotten that this is the way things work for us, here.

I think back to the list of things I like, I try to apply it to what it has been like, so far, living here. I like the canals, I think, I like having water around me. I like how Robin is here, how contented, how at ease. I labour to amplify.

I told him that I'm itchy here, that I feel the lack of movement. Forward motion, I intoned, and felt the breath of that hectoring workshop leader over my shoulder, the fluff of her pen tickling my ear. I'm not as inventive, I told Robin, as I thought.

You mean, he said, you're not as resourceful. And that's not true. I told him, carefully, that perhaps it was. Or perhaps I just needed something else, something different, from which to draw that resource.

Different people, he said, I get that. Of course I do. Of course he does, in a way.

When he asked, Where next? I could give no clear answer; though we knew, both of us, that the choice is hardly limited: there is back, and there is a type of forward, which means staying here, perhaps another city, and then there is the rest of the dubious world, where we have, as yet, no claim of work or money or relationships, no urgency of attraction. Not here, not the same again, and not what we've done before, I told him. Then I said I had to go out.

Well: this careful rootlessness, this artful lack of an origin story. Everywhere now there are people ferociously defending, defining their lives through the clinging sediment of culture, which can be poured from a chipped ladle, tacked to a pastel-painted wall, tugged on in the morning over tautly pleased skin, spoken in low-ceilinged rooms, felt in the hands and, by osmosis, in the heart. The personal spells woven about me have no such power, and consequently breed a poor guardian – what would I be so desperate to defend? And if you probed what that limp, grey dish, personal culture, actually meant, when applied to me, what would you find? A tasteless mâché of local news, wet leaves, hamsters, milk, trains snaking through unbothered territories, bland, perilous conversation, fumes and silence. It's hard to feel passionately about this, and part of my own breed of nostalgia is sorrow for a past that wasn't more mystical, or more hard-won.

It's more personal than this, of course. I feel the absence, the lack of grip, so acutely because I cannot provide the answering, necessary friction. I can't catch at the idea of— what? Culture, heritage, history, place – and make something sustaining out of it; these thoughts just glide through me, so interesting as I endlessly, mindlessly, intone, but with no headier allure. I don't know what it is.

I am tired of being stuck in the runnels of my own mind, a psychology I can't outrun, can only (sporadically) out-trick. And though my sharpest inner self can sit me up in the morning, whispering sourly: You have an indolent streak a mile wide – I don't think it's just that. What else? Embarrassment? Lack of permission? Girl, I think, how tragic.

I walked by the side of the canal, fists tight against the seams of my jacket pockets. Too warm, I realised too late, to be wearing this many layers. Bikes sped past me, their wheels within a few millimetres of the white line separating them from the pedestrian channel. One raced past, a woman balanced on the carrier, as I do sometimes with Robin, her arms clamped around the rider's waist. My best moments here have been sitting on the back of a bike, I realised, my hands tight around Robin's waist, as we cycle back from a party. Helmetless, I would lift my head up and watch the dark sky moving above me, a faint giddiness in my stomach, my knees held up, primly, to avoid the spokes as the bike swerves neatly across the gravel paths. I tell myself, in that moment, that this is the thing I will remember; the brief sensation that is specific to a time and place, to a person. I know I'll never travel like that again.

Acknowledgements

Thank you to Louise, Laura, Sarah and the rest of the team at Fairlight Books for seeing something in *Temper*, and helping me to see it as well. Special thanks to my skilful editor, Daniela Ferrante, who has worked with such care, intelligence and enthusiasm to bring *Temper* into its final, fully fledged form.

Thank you to the Society of Authors, whose Eric Gregory Award meant I was able to take some much-needed time to work on the manuscript in April 2022.

Thank you to my parents, Judy and Peter; and to Laurence, Angus and Laura, for their unflagging interest and encouragement. You are all good with words.

My last and largest thank you, as always, is to Sam.

About the Author

Phoebe Walker is originally from Northumberland. She has lived in both London and the Netherlands and is now based in Manchester, where she works as a development consultant. Her debut poetry pamphlet, *Animal Noises*, received an Eric Gregory Award in 2021. Phoebe also won the Mairtín Crawford Poetry Award in 2019 and a Northern Writers' Award for poetry in 2012. Her arts criticism has appeared in the *TLS* and the *Observer* and was shortlisted for the Observer/Anthony Burgess prize 2020. Phoebe's poetry has been published in *Ambit, Under the Radar, The Tangerine, The Moth, Magma* and was included in the Northern Poetry Library's 'Poem of the North' exhibition. *Temper* is her debut novel.